Tea & Trouble

A Cozy Witch Mystery

Book Store Cozy Mystery Series
Book 3

Lucinda Race

MC Two Press

Contents

Author's Note

Hi and welcome to my world of cozy mystery. I hope you love my characters as much as I do. So, turn the page and happy sleuthing .

If you'd like to stay in touch, please join my Newsletter. I release it twice per month with tidbits, recipes and an occasional special gift just for my readers so sign up here: https://lucindarace.com/newsletter/ and there's a free cozy mystery when you join!

Happy reading…

Pembroke Cove, ME

1. Robin's Cafe
2. Bygone Antiques
3. The Pembroke Cliffs
4. Cozy Nook Bookstore
5. Twisted Scissors Hair Salon
6. Betty's Market
7. Old Town Library
8. Miss Judy's Dance Studio
9. The Sweet Spot Baker
10. Bee Bee's Boutique
11. Tuckers Hardware Store
12. The Copper Kettle
13. Police Station
14. Town Hall

Editor Trish Long, Blossoming Pages
Cover design by Mariah Sinclair

Manufactured in the United States of America
First Edition August 2023

Print Edition ISBN 978-1-954520-48-6
E-book ISBN 978-1-954520-47-9

Chapter 1
Lily

QUICK NOTE: If you enjoy Tea & Trouble, be sure to check out my offer for a FREE bonus at the end. With that, happy reading!

I tilted my head back, face toward the early morning sun, and drank in the crisp fall air. It was a perfect day for the annual, seaside, Pembroke Cove Fall Festival. Today I was reading fortunes at my parents' tea booth. I slowly twirled in my long deep-burgundy velvet dress. The hem of the matching cloak brushed the tops of my black ankle boots as Gage Erikson, my best friend and hopefully someday my boyfriend, touched my hand. I wanted to look the part of a witch but I didn't want to wear all black. Aunt Mimi had found this dress in an old wooden trunk which had been tucked away, unopened, in her attic for years. The bonus, it was a perfect fit, as if it was made for me. I know my aunt thought it was kismet and even with being a witch, it didn't mean everything in life I touched was magical.

"Lily, you look beautiful." Gage's hand warmed mine, and his smile was the real deal.

I did a mini curtsy. "Thank you, sir." My heart skipped a beat as I took in his long, lean frame, well-trimmed, light-brown hair, and hazel eyes which were enhanced by the green flannel shirt he was wearing. Was that part of his costume? All the people working the festival agreed to stick with the theme of their booths. "I thought you were on duty today. What made you come up with dressing like a farmer in overalls and flannel?"

"I'm helping Marshall Stone with his stand." He pointed just across the town square. "I'll be right over there, and we can make funny faces at each other all day just like we did when we were in school."

I couldn't help but laugh at the way his eyebrows wiggled when he talked. "We're not twelve anymore." Sadly, that was twenty-five years ago. He twirled me again and this time he pulled me closer to his chest. He looked into my eyes with an intensity I hadn't seen before.

"After the last six weeks, I think we should go back to when we were kids and didn't have anything more to worry about than fishing and going to a movie at the Lights Out Theatre. Two murders and me getting crushed under that sign at the Clam Shack has been a lot to handle." Concern clouded his eyes. "And you did most of the heavy lifting."

I flashed him a cautious grin. I wasn't sure if he was referring to me levitating the sign off his body—which he still didn't know I actually did—or the fact that I was directly involved in solving the murders of Flora Gray and Teddy Roberts. With a nonchalant shrug, I said, "It was no big deal. I like puzzles and both of those incidents were a way to exercise my brain."

He leaned in and kissed my cheek like he always did

while he said, for my ears alone, "My best friend is brilliant."

And there it was, the perpetual friend zone. Would Gage ever look at me as more than his friend? Probably not. This had been going on for years. Maybe it was time I started dating someone else. Possibly Dax Peters, the investigator who had come to town around the time Flora was killed. He seemed to be showing more than a passing interest in me lately.

Before I could respond to his compliment, I noticed my parents headed in our direction. Dad was carrying a cardboard box which presumably held paper teacups and other supplies for brewing various teas and my mother had a tote bag slung over her shoulder with what I guessed would be her special blend. My aunt had told me Dad was a witch, but my mom wasn't. However, her tea blends were amazing, and today I would be reading tea leaves from a special blend she had created just for the festival. In addition, she had bags of other teas to sell in our booth.

I tugged my hand from his. "I need to help my parents. They brought more supplies for the booth."

"I'll come too." He fell in step beside me, and it was just one of the reasons he was a good guy, always ready to lend a hand. "Did Mindy make her special blend again this year?"

I gave him a quick side-glance. "You never miss a trick, do you?"

He puffed up his chest and strutted a bit. "It's my job, ma'am, to notice the little details as a detective on Pembroke Cove's police force."

I laughed so hard a snort escaped. "Easy, Detective. You might strain the buttons on your flannel shirt."

My parents met us halfway, and Gage took the bag from over my mother's shoulder and the box Dad was carrying.

"Hello, Reed." He gave my mom a one-armed hug. "Mindy." He looked at me. "Doesn't Lily look great in her witch costume?"

Dad's brow quirked at the word costume. Mom placed a gentle hand on his arm and said, "She looks amazing."

Mom reached out and straightened my modified witch hat. "I like how you decorated the traditional black hat with burgundy lace and cutouts of teacups."

"A touch of whimsy, Mom." I linked arms with hers and we crunched over a colorful blanket of red, yellow and orange leaves to our booth space. Parked behind the tables was a tiny silver camper from the 1970s. It was one my parents used every time they went to fairs in the northeast. Inside, we could heat water, get warm if the day was chilly, and if the day turned hot, cool off. And the best part was the fridge was always stocked with snacks.

Mom scanned the table setup. "I see you have everything ready to go."

"There wasn't much to do. You had it organized inside. All that was needed was to flick out the tablecloth, put cushions on the seats, and set out the bags of tea that you want to sell." I held up one hand and announced. "Voila."

Gage said, "Just like magic."

I leaned closer to Mom, and she wrapped her arm around my body. I whispered, "He doesn't know."

She nodded and conveyed her understanding with a concerned smile. Mom had known for years I was in love with Gage, even if he didn't. But I had come to terms with our relationship, and for the most part accepted we would always be best friends even if it wouldn't lead to anything more.

"Looks like it's going to be a great day for a festival," Dad said. "Gage, are you joining us in our booth this year?"

"No, sir. I volunteered to work at Marshall's booth. His helper got food poisoning, and Marshall needs an extra set of hands." He set the box and bag on the corner of the display table. "Is there more in the truck?"

Dad nodded. "Ladies, we'll be back."

They started off in the direction of vendor parking, and Mom began to unpack the bagged tea. "Are you ever going to tell Gage that you care for him as more than a friend?"

I picked up a sleeve of paper teacups and began to set them up next to the bag of loose-leaf tea I would use for the readings. Longing to say yes, instead I looked away and said, "No. He doesn't think of me in that way."

Mom quirked a brow. "Are you sure about that?"

I looked at him walking next to Dad. "He's had so many opportunities and never said anything."

"Neither have you." It was a gentle rebuke, but I was a bit old-fashioned and thought the man should state his feelings first. Like Gage asking me on a real date. Not like the casual, *hey, let's have dinner tonight,* kind of comment.

"We're better off as friends. If we started dating, it might not work out, and then I'd lose what we have."

"That's not like you, Lily, leaning in to the fear of the unknown. You've always been an eternal optimist." She smoothed my hair back from my face and searched my eyes. "Do you want to talk about what is really going on?"

Maintaining eye contact, I said, "I've made a decision to start dating. I might even ask Dax Peters if he'd like to have coffee with me." That went against my idea of dating, but those rules only applied to Gage.

Mom's hand cupped my cheek and she kissed the other one. "I think that is a fine idea. Get out there and have some fun."

I saw the sparkle that came into her deep-brown eyes as

she spoke. "Mom, do you sense something that I should know?"

Her smile quirked as she laughed. "My intuition is not sparking today, at least not yet, but give it time. With all the witches who will be wandering around the town green today, it might."

"We haven't really talked about me finally discovering I'm a witch. But I don't understand—why doesn't Dad practice his craft like Aunt Mimi?"

Mom didn't answer right away as she finished setting out the items we would sell today. Once she was assured everything was to her satisfaction, she spoke softly. "We always thought I would grow into my powers, but I didn't. I've learned to accept that I have a strong intuition and a talent for blending tea. Your father, being a kind and wonderful husband, put aside the use of his powers for me. Reed knew I felt bad we didn't share that special gift. And for the longest time we believed you were like me. Rather than have you feel like you had missed out on something wonderful, we remained silent. It might not have been the best idea since you may have gained your powers sooner. But we can't change the past."

"Mom. Dad adores you, and whatever decision he made, he did with an open heart. I'm not sorry I didn't find out sooner since we have no way of knowing what kind of mischief I could have gotten into being a witch at a much younger age. I don't have much control now based on how I struggle with even the basic spells."

"You and Nikki would have had more to talk about." She looked over my shoulder and a smile graced her lips. The one she reserved for my father.

"Don't you worry; we've never lacked for conversation." I gave her a quick hug. "Now, let's finish getting ready.

Customers will soon be flocking to our booth to buy your tea, and with any luck, I'll get a few people who want their leaves read."

Mom tipped her head to the side and held my hands. Her gaze burned into my soul. "Trust your instincts. They won't let you down. Above all, tell the truth on what you see. Lives will be changed today."

At a loss for words, all I could do was nod. She dropped my hands and turned to smile at Gage and Dad. The moment passed as a shiver raced down my arms. I ran my hands over them, determined to chase away the chill that had settled over me.

"I'm going to check on Milo. I'll be right back."

Gage set down the box. "Do you want company?"

I needed to spend a few minutes alone with my familiar. "I'll just be a minute, but we'll touch base later."

He said, "Okay."

It was easy to see he didn't think anything was amiss. I hurried across the grass in the direction of the crosswalk when shouting from the direction of Dean Hartley's booth drew my attention, causing me to slow my steps. He was shouting, his arms gesturing wildly at a man I didn't recognize at first. Dean took a step back, and when he did, I saw it was Mike Shaw. He owned the garden center on the south side of town and was a founding member of the Pembroke Cove Garden Club. Dean's face was bright red, and he was shaking a fist at Mike's face. When Mike said something else, there was another angry eruption before Dean turned his back on Mike. He threw up his hands and stalked away. It was good that one of the men had the sense to stop the argument. People in the town square were starting to look in their direction. I crossed the street and stepped on the brick sidewalk and withdrew the large brass key from my pocket to unlock the door. My bookshop, it wasn't just my business, but also my sanctuary where my cat and familiar, Milo, hung out during the day with me and where I read my book of spells, *Practical Beginnings*.

"Milo?" I called out and checked the window seat, which was one of his favorite places to snooze. When he wasn't there, I went in the direction of the children's corner to another one of his hidey-holes. There was my gray bundle of fur. I scooped him up, rousing him from a deep sleep.

"Hey, fur ball. Wake up. I need to ask you a question." I cradled him in my arms as I hurried to the front counter. He squirmed as I placed him down, and once seated, he began to lick his front paw, doing his best to ignore me.

"I need your advice."

"What else is new?" he grumbled as he glanced at me before going back to his grooming.

"I get the feeling something bad is going to happen today."

Finally, he stopped and gave me his best bored look. In his deep kitty growl, he asked, "What's the problem?"

"Mom told me when I read the leaves today, to be honest about what I see. That it will change lives."

"And you decided to jump to a conclusion that it had to be bad. What has gotten into you, my dear witch?"

I crossed my arms over my chest and tapped the toe of my black pointy ankle boot. Milo could be exasperating, and why did he pick now to do so? "It wasn't what she said, but how she said it. All serious."

"Maybe someone is going to win money today or find their life partner." He rose to all four paws and did a long and lazy stretch. "This is the first year you've read tea leaves as a witch, and you read the book, right?"

I nodded.

"It doesn't mean you have the gift to do that too. So far, we can't pin down where you fit in the overall witch category. Do your best, and we'll talk about it all tonight. And since you woke me from a very nice fish dream, we should have cod for dinner. And maybe ask Detective Cutie to join us."

Not bothering to keep the exasperation from my voice, I said, "Stop calling Gage that, and I'll think about swinging by the dock to purchase fish." I dropped a quick kiss on his soft gray head and hurried to the door. So much for my familiar guiding me.

Business was brisk at our booth as shoppers purchased tea, and a steady stream of customers wanted to sit with me as well. I had been reading tea leaves all day, and so far, nothing out of the ordinary happened. I gave everyone happy things to look forward to. As the crowd was starting to thin, I leaned back in the chair and closed my eyes. I hated to admit it, but I was on the edge of exhaustion. One more hour and we could shut it down for another year. I was curious why this year had been particularly draining. Did it have anything to do with me knowing I was a witch?

A raucous commotion disturbed my break. I opened my eyes and looked around before I locked my attention on Dean Hartley's flower booth. He was having another shouting match with Tucker Gleason, the owner of the hardware store. I watched as Tucker grabbed a pair of hedge shears from Dean and shook his head in obvious disgust. Red-faced, Dean stopped yelling and handed over what looked like money to Tucker, who walked away, leaving the tool behind.

As if that altercation hadn't happened, Mike Shaw approached the flower display. I braced myself for a repeat performance from Mike, but then he shook Dean's hand and clasped his other hand on top of Dean's, giving it a hearty shake as if the skirmish from earlier never happened. As he pumped Dean's hand, he was beaming and then gestured to the blue ribbons that adorned pots of roses on display. Dean jerked his hand away and took a step back. Then he pointed in the direction of the parking area, and Mike shook his head.

I sat up straighter. This was curious. At first, it seemed they had set aside their differences. Even good friends could have a minor argument. A woman approached my table requesting a reading. Distracted, I began the process of making the tea. She drank some and then swirled the cup and turned it upside down. Another good one. I smiled as I gave her an optimistic reading—when I really longed to watch the excitement across the park.

After I had finished with my customer, commotion from Dean's booth once again broke out. This time a group of people were clustered around the roses and I could hear raised voices but not specifically what was being said. A woman, whom I recognized as Edie Jenkins, was poking him in the chest, pushing Dean back with each jab. She was a regular in my bookstore for gardening books, but I had never seen her temper before. I got up from my chair and strolled in the general direction of the group gathering in front of the flower display. I was attempting to get close without appearing as if I was eavesdropping once I got within hearing distance of the booth. Whatever was happening over there wasn't good. Before I got close enough to hear, I saw Ava Springs, a good friend of Edie's, shouting at Dean. Alvin, Ava's brother, was lingering in the back.

They were all members of the same garden club so why on earth was everyone so riled up?

"Dean," I called out. "We're going to close up soon, and you mentioned you wanted to purchase some tea." Everyone stopped grumbling as I drew closer.

He gave me a confused look, and then he seemed to understand I was trying to help him get off the hot seat he was on. "Yes, thank you, Lily, for the reminder." He pushed his way through the group and escorted me back to the tea booth.

"How about a cup of tea too. Looks like you could use a pick-me-up."

He gave me a funny grin. "Maybe you should read the leaves. Everyone is talking about the great fortunes that you've bestowed on them after a cup." His grin turned into a scowl as he glanced over his shoulder. "I could use some good news right about now."

Chapter 2
Lily

Dean settled into the chair across from me as I filled the teacup with hot water to steep the loose-leaf tea. "Tell me what you'd like to know." I studied him intently, wondering if he was looking for love or money.

Without hesitation, he said, "Peace and quiet. Solitude."

I looked in the direction of his flower booth. "Things seemed to get heated over there a few times today." I swung my attention back to him, more curious than concerned about what had happened.

"Yeah. A few people are mad about a hybrid rose I grew. Said I stole it, which I didn't."

That was an odd statement. I could hear my voice perk up as I asked, "Like, stole a bush?"

His shoulders drooped as he shook his head and leaned back in the folding chair. Crossing his arms over his chest, he lifted his chin and asked, "How much do you know about rose propagation?"

"Very little." I leaned forward, glanced at the steeping tea, and looked back to Dean.

"Here's the thing. You can't just take a cutting from any rose you like and grow it. Some are protected by patents." He must have seen the confused look on my face before he said, "Think of it this way. Someone put a lot of effort, time, and money into developing a new hybrid rose and they want to protect it so they can get the return on their investment before hacks start selling replicas. Cuttings shouldn't be taken and propagated for personal gain. It's stealing. A few people in this town think that's how I got my new hybrid rose." He snorted and a look of annoyance settled into the lines on his face. "Can you imagine, me stealing."

The last sentence he said more to himself than to me. It wasn't my place to come right out and ask him if that is what he did. However, by the sounds of everyone today, it was certainly the working theory.

He jabbed his finger in the direction of the teacup. "Is that ready? I need to get back to my booth to clean up. I'm going to cut out early."

I gave him a small smile as I handed the paper cup to him, instructing him to drink the tea, being careful to leave bits of the leaves in the bottom. Dean did as I asked and handed the cup back to me. I took it in my left hand, swirled what was left of the brew, and turned it upside down on a paper towel. "Dean. Please place your hands on the cup and with clear thoughts, concentrate on what you would like to know."

I waited for a long minute while he thought. Finally, he looked up. "Can I remove my hands now?"

"Yes." I flipped the cup over with the paper handle facing left. Pulling the towel off the top, the wet leaves dropped back into the cup, then I discarded the paper. Peering inside on the upper half were some leaves but the bulk were in the bottom and shaped like a broken sword. I searched my memory for what I had read in the tea leaf reading book that Milo had insisted I peruse before today, but all I could remember was swords were a bad omen.

"What's wrong? I can see you're frowning." Dean peered into the cup. "Is there something I should know about?"

I exhaled slowly. I certainly wasn't about to tell him that a broken sword was one of the worst things I had seen today so I tempered it. "I'm seeing that people have been upset with you today."

I lifted my head as he narrowed his eyes. "I didn't need tea to tell me that."

I pointed to the upper left half of the cup. "These represent from today through the next three months. And see how the leaves look like a sword? That means you'll have more disagreements. However, you need to take care that whoever you disagree with doesn't get the upper hand. It could indicate a bad outcome for you."

"Like it might hurt my business?" He took the cup from me. "How come most of the leaves seem to be in the one section?"

"I'm not sure specifically but try to work with people, not against them." A stiff ocean breeze raced over me, and I couldn't shake the feeling that this had to be my last customer for today. Reading tea leaves started out as a lark, but this—I took another look at Dean's cup—this was borderline sinister.

"Why couldn't you have told me I was about to come into money? Instead of a sword." He pushed back his chair and got up and looked at my mother. "Mindy, any chance I can swing back after I pack up my booth and get two bags of the sunshine blend?"

Mom seemed surprised with the order, but she quickly

composed her friendly saleswoman smile. "I'll put two of today's special aside for you."

"Great, thanks." He handed her a twenty-dollar bill and me a ten. "Will that cover my reading and the tea?"

I nodded and gave Dean my best upbeat smile. "Thank you. Enjoy the rest of your day."

He grunted and moved away as I sank into my chair, wanting to disappear. "Mom. I'm done for today. Out of everyone I did, Dean's was the only one that I messed up. I must be tired."

Mom slipped into the chair where Dean had sat. She looked at his cup without touching it. "What is it?"

I closed my eyes and tipped my head back, hoping the sun would replace the chill that had settled over me. "To me it looks like he's in for a heap of trouble in the coming months. I suggested he try to get along with others, but I don't think he heard me."

"Lily. Do you really think you saw something bad? You've been working this festival for years, but until this year you've always had fun."

"That was before I found out I was a witch and could cast spells." My eyes felt like sandpaper as I rubbed them with the back of my hands. "Do you think now that I've been learning spells, this could have taken on a different meaning?"

She took my hands and warmth radiated from her directly to my heart, lifting my spirit. "Your aunt Mimi would be better equipped to answer that question. Why don't you see if you can find her?"

I gave Mom a grin. "I can do better than that; I've learned a summoning spell." I closed my eyes and murmured under my breath, *Aunt Mimi, I need your help. Come to me, and so it shall be.* When I opened my eyes,

Mom was scanning the people milling about the park, and a smile slid from one side of her face to the other.

"If I hadn't watched your concentration, I might not have known for sure." She nodded behind me, but I didn't need to look. I could feel my aunt's positive energy radiating in my direction. When she reached us, Aunt Mimi placed a warm, comforting hand on my shoulder. It wasn't until we connected that I understood how drained I had become. Her presence boosted my mood even higher when combined with Mom's hand on my arm.

She kept her eyes on my mother. "Hi, Mindy. Have sales been brisk today?"

"Mimi, it's so good to see you as always, and I put some tea aside for you." She got up from the chair and gestured for my aunt to sit down. "I'll leave you and Lily to talk, and Reed will pack a bag for you."

Aunt Mimi smiled, and I could see a reflection of myself sitting in the chair across from me. We had the same brown eyes, both petite and a smattering of freckles and before her hair turned silver it had been chestnut brown. "Lily?"

Without any preamble, I launched into my question. "Do you think I'm really able to read tea leaves or is it more of a kitchen witch thing, like should Nikki be doing this and not me?"

Her smile stayed on her face and filled her sable-brown eyes with warmth. The gloom that had settled over me was completely gone. "There is one thing I know about your gift —it is constantly evolving. I don't believe you fit into any one category, which I find fascinating. You may have been honing this particular skill all these years without ever real-izing it." She tipped her head. "Tell me what you saw that has upset you."

"A broken sword in Dean Hartley's cup."

"I see." Aunt Mimi pursed her lips, and her gaze drifted to where he was packing up crates of potted plants on a flat wagon. "What else did you see?"

"Nothing. Everything was in the short-term section of the cup. And I know what you're thinking."

Her brow shot to her graying hairline. "You do? Then tell me."

"I shouldn't have used paper cups and this was nothing more than using inferior supplies. In addition, I was unduly influenced by the people he has been fighting with off and on today. And I'm not a kitchen witch and have no business reading leaves and next year I should leave it to my best friend, Nikki, who would be so much better at this than me." My shoulders sagged toward the ground as I finished my woe-is-me speech.

"Hmm. None of that had crossed my mind. What had, is your mother's intuition. Did you ask her what she might think?"

"No." To my ears, I sounded like a petulant child. "When I mentioned what I had seen, she suggested I talk to you."

She nodded. "Interesting." With a pat on my hand, she got up. "Try not to fret, Lily. I'm sure it's nothing, and if something comes to pass, we'll talk again." With a kiss on my cheek, she said, "I'm going to wander around. Stop by my place tomorrow for lunch, and we will talk about this more in depth."

Relieved, I got up and wrapped my arms around her, holding her tight. "Thank you. Talking with you always makes me feel much better."

"Lily, you need to be patient with yourself. You've been trying to catch up on years of training in mere weeks. And you're still finding your way. I promise all the puzzle pieces will fall into place given sufficient time." With a flutter of Aunt Mimi's hands, the paper cups and plates slid into the trash can.

One day I hoped to be able to do that spell. It would make cleaning my house a breeze.

"The festival is almost over. Call it a day, and find your detective. Having dinner with him will be good for you both." Aunt Mimi retrieved her bag of tea from Dad and crossed the green to where Gage was handing a paper shopping bag to a customer. By the looks of Marshall's almost empty flat wagon, it had been a good day for him too.

Thirty minutes later, we had the teas packed and boxes had been stored inside the camper for the trip back to my parents'. And one additional box was ready to go to my bookshop since my tea display was running low.

My mom held up a brown paper bag and a frown flicked over her face as she scanned the park. "Would you look at that. Dean packed up his booth and didn't come back for his order. Your father and I are going straight home with the camper, but I'll give him a call and tell him we'll drop the bag off tomorrow."

I held out my hand to her. "I'll take it to him." I looked over my shoulder and found who I was looking for, and I glanced at Mom. "I'll ask Gage if he wants to ride out to Dean's place with me."

Her smile spread across her face. "You could ask him to have dinner too. I bet he'd jump at the chance." She held up her hand and kept talking. "I know you said you were thinking of asking Dax out, but we both know who you'd really like sitting across a table from you."

She had a point, but I wasn't going to admit it. "Milo

said I should invite Gage to have dinner with us, and my furry familiar asked for fish. But on second thought, I'll stop at Dean's and then head home. You brought up a good point; I need to decide what I want regarding Dax."

She gently patted my cheek and nodded in Gage's direction. "What you need to do is go after the man who has always been by your side. Listen to your heart. You know deep down it's always been Gage."

Milo was stretched out and snoozing in the back of my car as I took the road leading to Pine Valley and away from the coast. Dean Hartley's home and greenhouse were about twenty minutes outside of town. I glanced at the passenger seat where the bag of teas he purchased sat. I was wishing I'd asked Nikki to ride with me. It was getting dark, and the road to his place was low traffic at any time of day. I slowed and pulled to the shoulder. I wasn't far from her place and who knows? Maybe she'd be up for an impromptu pizza on the way back.

Nikki answered on the second ring. "Hey, Lily. This is a surprise." Her voice was as bubbly as a shaken bottle of soda and sweet as honey at the same time.

"Hi. I'm headed out to Hartley's Greenhouse to drop off some tea Dean bought at the festival today. Any chance you want to come with me?"

"Sure. Steve went on a wrecker call and isn't back yet, and I'm just sitting here reading. When are you going to pick me up?"

"Five minutes?" I knew the timing wouldn't be a problem. Nikki was always up for any adventure with me, even one so mundane as delivering tea.

"Of course. I'll shoot him a text in case he gets home before me. See you in a few."

I pulled a U-turn in the road to make the short drive to Nikki's cottage. The moment I pulled up the driveway, she came out the back door. In one hand she carried a floral tin. My stomach rumbled in anticipation when I saw it was the one we passed back and forth with cookies she had baked. My role was her exclusive taste tester. Not that she needed someone to give her feedback. Her skills as a kitchen witch had helped her baking business thrive. I was always happy to get samples of her latest creations.

After she buckled up and handed me a cookie, and in between bites and groans of buttery goodness, I filled her in on my readings for the day. A couple customers' reactions left us laughing, and then I filled her in on my last one— Dean's and the sword complication.

Her eyes grew wide, and her smile faded away. "How did he take the news that he needed to be careful?"

"As you'd expect. He didn't take it seriously, but I don't know what to make of it. Unless I'm really bad at seeing fortunes in leaves, I studied the book Milo gave me, and it was distinct, like nothing I've ever seen in any cup before."

Her brows knitted together. "Hmm. And you said he was arguing with people throughout the day?"

"Mostly people from the garden club." I put my blinker on to turn onto the gravel road that led to his house. "Something about roses and grafting. He tried to explain it to me, but I still don't get why people would be so upset over a new variety of flower."

I double-checked that Milo was still snoozing before I took in the beautiful landscaping. If nothing else, Dean knew how to keep stunning gardens, and by the looks of the riot of fall colors in the flower beds that lined the driveway, it wasn't just roses he enjoyed growing. To the right were fruit trees and to the left the forest provided a buffer to the gardens, and there was a large greenhouse looming in front of us. I pulled into a parking space on the other side of the gravel drive and noticed the side door was standing open.

I half stepped inside the spacious building filled with row after row of rose plants and called out to Dean with no answer. I closed the door before we walked through an opening in the shrubs which stood eight feet tall on either side, creating a wall between the greenhouse and garden space beyond. "Dean?" I called out again. Shadows crept closer to us as we walked deeper into the garden.

A chill slithered down my spine, and I clutched the paper bag handles tighter. "Come on, Nikki, let's go this way." I was inexplicably drawn to the back side of the garden to another row of shrubs. A ladder was on the ground, and a large mound was lying next to it. My heartbeat kicked up as a lead weight filled my stomach. I knew it wasn't bags of mulch or peat moss lying there. I grabbed Nikki's arm and pulled her to my side. As we got near, her death grip on my arm stopped me from getting any closer. Dean was on his back, lying in a pool of coagulating blood, his wide eyes staring at the sky and the handles of hedge shears protruding from his upper abdomen. His waxy skin confirmed all I needed to know. Dean Hartley was dead.

Chapter 3
Gage

Lily's call had come as a total shock. She was at Dean Hartley's place and it sounded like he was dead after being impaled with garden shears. The only good thing about the situation was that she wasn't alone. Her best friend, Nikki, was with her.

I could hear the fear-tinged words as she said, "Gage, please hurry. He looks just awful with his eyes wide open and blood everywhere."

The anguish in her voice shattered my heart. "You and Nikki keep your distance and don't touch anything." I didn't want the shock of finding another dead person to overwhelm Lily. Even the strongest person could crumble under all she had dealt with. It was her third death in almost as many months, and I needed to get to her and fast. "I'll be there as soon as I can, and if anything spooks you, get back to the car and lock the doors." Lily had been blessed with a level head and logical thinking, and despite her tendency to err on the side of curiosity, she wouldn't take unnecessary chances.

"We'll be fine. Don't worry, Gage. Just hurry."

She had said goodbye, and I called in the information to the station. I requested my two best officers, Sharon Peabody and Mac Sullivan, to meet me at the scene. They had become invaluable since joining the police force, and it was my hope they wouldn't find any evidence of foul play at the Hartley place. I hoped it was an unfortunate accident. We didn't need another murder in Pembroke Cove.

Less than half an hour later, I parked my car next to a police cruiser and Lily's Mini Coop and noticed Milo was sitting in the driver's seat, his eyes locked on mine as if it was a gentle reproach for his mistress once again finding a dead body.

It reminded me of the time shortly after Lily adopted him and he was in the car when we had gone to talk to a kid about missing money from the Sweet Spot Bakery. Milo wore an all-knowing look that made me wish he could talk. I was sure he never missed a thing.

I jogged down the path and around the greenhouse in the direction to where I heard voices. Lily and Nikki were talking to Peabody and Mac. Relief washed over Lily's face the instant our eyes met.

In a steady voice, she said, "Gage. I was just going to tell Sharon and Mac what I knew."

Lily was the only person who got away with calling Peabody by her first name. "It's a good thing I got here so you only have to tell the story once." I gave Nikki a small smile. "Hey, how are you doing?"

She gave me a shaky smile. "I'm okay, but Lily is a rock. You'd think this was an everyday occurrence for her, discovering a dead person."

I looked to Peabody and Mac, both nodding their confirmation of the situation—Dean was dead. I extended my arm away from where crime scene tape was being run around a wide perimeter, gesturing for the ladies to follow me. Having them go with me solved two purposes—to divert their attention from Dean's body being moved and also, in my experience, bright-yellow tape was distracting.

I clasped Lily's hand in mine and looked her in the eye. "Are you sure you're okay?"

She glanced over her shoulder, her voice heavy with regret as she said, "If only we had gotten here sooner, we might have been able to help him when he slipped off the ladder." She shuddered. "Can you imagine how helpless and scared he must have felt lying there bleeding to death? And with no one close enough to hear his cries for help."

Tears welled up in her eyes, and before I could hand her my handkerchief, she wiped them away with the sleeve of her dress.

"Detective, would you come over here for a minute?" Mac called to me, his voice cool and professional, which led me to the conclusion he found something out of the ordinary.

I looked from Lily to Nikki. "Stay here." I didn't wait for them to answer, but in several long strides, I was next to Peabody where she knelt on the ground.

She rocked back on her heels. "Detective, Mac and I have come to a consensus." She pointed to the handles of the loppers. "If you look closely at the wounds and the angle of the blades, we believe it indicates they penetrated the body from a lower angle, thrust up. In addition, Lily and Nikki said they hadn't moved the body and that he was on his back. If he had fallen from the ladder, I would suspect he'd be facedown, potentially with a side puncture, not dead center."

Mac took two steps in the direction of the ladder. "Based on the body and the ladder being close and perpendicular to each other, the ladder was either placed next to the victim and he was never on it or Dean leapt away from it as he fell. But that doesn't fit with the way he is lying, and the ladder would have been extended."

I nodded and could see the scenarios in my mind based on what they were saying. But if someone had killed Dean, when and why? He might be a bit of a curmudgeon, but other than his membership in the garden club, he kept to himself for the most part. "Have you seen anything else that would support your theory?"

Lily cleared her throat. I wasn't surprised she and Nikki would get as close as they could once I had been called over. She held out a crumpled tissue and unfolded it. "After I called you to report finding Dean, Nikki and I were walking away from—well, you know. It was also like, with his eyes open, he was going to sit up and talk. But anyway, I found this bright-pink fake fingernail in the grass."

Peabody pulled a small evidence bag from the side pocket of her pants. This officer was always prepared, and I had a momentary thought she must have been a Scout when she was a kid. "I'm glad you used a tissue to pick the nail up. Can you place both items in this bag, please?"

Lily did as Peabody requested. "Do you know anyone who has long nails with this shade of pink?"

As Peabody sealed the bag, Lily was quiet. She was very observant, and with as many locals stopping into her bookshop and at the festival today, she might have noticed someone. It was a long shot as far as leads went, but it was better than nothing.

Her brow furrowed, and she closed her eyes for a minute as if she were rewinding a video and watching it. I wasn't about to rush her since this could be important evidence. "There was a woman who bought tea today after she had a mild argument with Dean, but I don't recall her having pink polish on her nails. Besides, it seemed like everyone who went to his booth had harsh words with him. I wouldn't put much stock in that."

"Do you know who the woman was?"

Lily didn't blink as she said, "Ava Springs."

"From the Pembroke Cove Garden Club?" Nikki asked. "She's an old, nosy Nellie but harmless."

"There were several people from the garden club who bought tea later in the afternoon. That was before Dean came to our booth. He bought some tea and asked for a reading." She held up a small brown paper bag. "He forgot it which is why I'm here. He's a good customer for my mother and likes her tea blends, and today it seemed the tea was the brightest spot in his day."

I crossed my arms over my chest and waited. "There has to be more to the story."

Lily paused while a gurney was wheeled closer to where Dean Hartley lay. She sucked in a breath, and Nikki turned away as his body was lifted from the ground, pruners still jutting from him, and wheeled to the waiting ambulance.

"Why didn't someone take those out of him? It seems cruel." Even though Lily was asking me a question, her eyes never left the cloth-draped gurney.

"Part of the autopsy is to determine how the pruners got lodged into his abdomen."

Nikki swayed and Lily slipped her arm around Nikki's waist, pulling her close. "This wasn't an accident?" Her voice was controlled and her eyes wide as they strayed to where the body had been.

I would like to have put my arms around Lily, but I hesitated. Nikki's face had gone white, but not Lily. She supported Nikki while keeping her back ramrod straight, waiting for my answer. "That's what the autopsy will tell us." I touched her arm, and she looked at me.

"Do you think this has anything to do with Teddy's real estate scheme? Maybe someone wanted to buy Dean's land and he wasn't selling."

Dang, her mind was quick. In fact, faster than mine since I hadn't thought of that angle. It had only been a couple of weeks before that someone murdered Teddy Roberts and I discovered he had been tied up in shady real estate deals that were not yet solved. "I won't know until we have answers from the medical examiner and we finish our investigation here."

Her eyes grew even wider. "I can help."

I chuckled. "I'm sure you would be invaluable to the investigation, but leave the police work to the professionals this time, please." I dropped my arm around her shoulders and gently steered her and Nikki in the direction of her car. "Take Milo home, give him some catnip, and call it a day." I dropped a friendly kiss on her forehead. "I'll swing by tomorrow, and we'll catch up."

"Is that a euphemism for, you'll tell me all you know about the case?"

"No. That means we can talk about your tea reading skills. Maybe I should have you read mine."

Her smile dimmed, and it slipped into a frown. "I think I'm getting out of the leaf reading business."

That was an odd thing for Lily to say. "Why?"

"When Dean bought the tea, he asked for a reading."

She stopped talking, leaving me hanging for what else had transpired. I wasn't sure tea leaves could predict a person's future, but many people around Pembroke Cove did and it behooved me to keep an open mind. "And?" I applied gentle pressure to her hand to get her to look at me.

With a slight tremor in her voice, she said, "I saw a broken sword."

Her sable-brown eyes had grown wide, and I knew Lily was a person who felt these types of readings were accurate. "You didn't cause this tragedy to happen."

A flicker of annoyance flashed in her eyes. "I know that. But I should have taken what I saw more seriously. If I had, Dean might have, and he'd be alive instead of being driven to the morgue with pruning shears sticking out of his belly."

I needed to tread carefully so as not to offend Lily and still reassure her this had nothing to do with tea. "People will believe, or not, whatever they want. You gave Dean the reading and what did he do or say?"

"He asked why I couldn't predict he was going to come into money instead of the sword." She rubbed her hands over her jacket sleeves as if she was chilled. The air had cooled as the sun had dipped behind the line of pine trees.

"Go home, and I'll see you tomorrow."

"Better yet, come for breakfast. I'll make waffles and bacon, extra crispy just the way you like them."

Now she was playing dirty. Lily knew I could never turn down her waffles and bacon. And we both knew it was one of her specialties.

I glanced at Nikki. "Why don't you and Steve come over too." There was no way Lily would drill me about the case with Nikki and her fiancé at the same table. Afterward maybe, but at least I could buy some time. My instincts were on overdrive; if I wasn't careful, the lovely Lily would be smack-dab in the middle of my murder investigation, and this time her luck might run out.

Nikki looked from me to Lily and back again. "Sounds

great and I'll bake something savory to go along with the sweet that Lily's going to whip up."

"Good. I'll be at Lily's at eight thirty if that works for you ladies."

Lily gave me a playful poke in my chest. "And if you get hung up at work, be prepared to share all the details." She looked around me as the doors closed on the back of the ambulance. "I know you don't want me anywhere near this case, but since I had a front row seat to most of Dean's day, I think I'm one of the best people to help you work through this puzzle."

I longed to wrap Lily in Bubble Wrap for her own protection, but all she would do is burst it to gain her freedom so she could do what she loved best—solve riddles.

"How about we make a deal?" I could see the gleam in her eyes.

"Go on, I'm listening."

I shook my head, wondering how I usually got into the situation where I was bargaining with a very pretty but smart bookstore owner about a case. "If you don't start asking people questions tonight and give me a chance to investigate, maybe I'll give you a few of the details that won't be in the newspaper."

She tipped her head to the side and grinned. "You're going to give me just enough to make me think I'm helping, when in fact it will be like tasting the chocolate chip cookie batter, but not letting me have a fresh baked cookie with a cold glass of milk."

Now I couldn't help but let out a loud laugh. "Cooking analogies from you? Nikki, yes, but you hate baking."

She sniffed and tried to look hurt but instead she giggled. "I may hate baking, but I've watched Nikki enough times and tasted enough cookie dough to know how it all fits together." She stood on tiptoes and kissed my cheek and then said only loud enough for me to hear, "You know I'm going to find out who did what and why. Wouldn't it be easier if you just shared all your information with me?"

I shook my head. "No. Again, murder means there is a murderer, and the last two times, with Flora Gray and Teddy Roberts, you got lucky. I was able to get to you before anyone hurt you. If you get involved again, our luck might run out, and I would never forgive myself if something happened to you."

Her eyes grew wide, and she sucked in an audible gasp. "Gage, what are you saying?"

Here was the opening I had been waiting for. The perfect time to tell Lily that I was in love with her.

"Detective?" Peabody called to me. "A word?"

Lily let out a ragged exhale, and disappointment flashed across her face.

Was that from relief or regret we had been interrupted? "I gotta go." I bobbed my head to where Dean had been lying only moments before. "We'll talk tomorrow?"

She nodded, and her shoulders sagged. "Yes. At breakfast."

I opened my mouth to say, *I love you*, even though this was not the time or place, but again, I heard, "Detective." Only this time it was Mac, and the urgency in his voice caused me to turn away. I took one step and stopped, turning back to Lily. "Text me you got home okay?"

"I will." She wrapped her arms around her waist. "This really wasn't an accident, was it?"

I gave her a hard look and decided no answer was the best one I could give her at this time.

Chapter 4
Lily

The next morning, I surveyed the kitchen, satisfied with my progress. The waffle batter was mixed and in the refrigerator, and the table was set, so I pulled out my sidewalk chalkboard from the pantry closet, which I had come to think of as my clue board.

Milo stalked into the room and glared at me. "Lily," he grumbled, "if you had wanted to hang out forever at a crime scene, you should have brought me home first."

Finally, he decided to talk to me. Since last night, he had given me the silent treatment. I wondered when I was going to get used to the fact that my cat talked and he was my familiar. He was supposed to teach me about being a witch, but his recurring comment was to read the big book, *Practical Beginnings*. "Milo, I'm sorry you were upset. I didn't expect to be at Dean Hartley's place that long. I had no idea I'd find him dead. I was delivering tea. Besides, you've been with me before while investigating."

He jumped with ease to the kitchen chair and gave me a cool stare. I flinched under his gaze. It was like being scolded by my fifth-grade teacher. "What now?"

"That isn't quite the truth. I've investigated and passed information to you, but Nikki is your partner in sleuthing. And don't confuse us, I'm much better looking than the blue eyed blond." He began to wash his front paw and ignore me.

If the situation wasn't so comical, I would have come back with a sharp retort. Instead, I focused my attention on the chalkboard and jotted down what I remembered from the festival. It had been less than twenty-four hours, but it seemed like weeks had passed.

There were four people who had argued with Dean, and of course at the end of the day, the garden club group had all jumped into the fray. I thought of Gage. Would he confirm it was murder and not an accident since my instincts were screaming it was murder?

I jotted down the members of the garden club and took a step back. Satisfied that was everyone I could remember, I said, "Milo, will you look at my list of suspects?"

Without stopping his face cleaning, he asked, "Why? You had me locked up in the bookstore all day."

I laughed. "And you didn't use the kitty door at all yesterday?"

He scoffed, "And if I did?"

I sighed. Sometimes he was exasperating. "If you had gone out and wandered around, could you have seen these people wandering around the festival? Is there any possibility of someone else that I overlooked?"

"Turn the board this way and let me have a look." He gave me a slow wink. "And it's a very good thing you are in the company of a multitalented and forgiving familiar. Not all of us can read, you know."

That was a new tidbit. "I didn't." I rubbed the top of his downy head while he perused my list.

He asked, "Did Hartley argue with Tucker Gleason?"

"It was pretty minor, but things were more animated with Edie Jenkins and Ava Springs. And over the course of the argument, Alvin got involved too. I think he was trying to plump up his image for Edie, since she is a single lady in the club and of course he'd defend his sister."

"Strutting his stuff so to speak." He scanned the list again. "I saw Mike Shaw arguing with Dean when he was setting up early in the morning. It didn't seem to be death threat intense, but you should add him to the suspect list."

I had forgotten him and jotted his name down and then tapped my chin, trying to recall if I had seen Mike later in the day. "I didn't notice him after that altercation."

Milo hopped off the chair. "You were busy all day and couldn't see everything at all times." He stalked to the kitchen door and glared at me with a haughty look. "Put the chalkboard away before your company arrives and save me some bacon."

He always seemed to know what I needed to do before I did. I slid the chalkboard in the pantry and before I could close the closet, the back door swung open. Nikki and Steve breezed in, each carrying a basket, and Gage brought up the rear. After we exchanged good mornings, Nikki pulled a quiche from her basket, and Steve placed a plate of scones on the table. Gage set a vase of fall flowers in the center.

The house was filled with wonderful sweet and savory aromas and it was time to cook the waffles so we could enjoy the mini feast. I did have a slight ulterior motive to hurry; I wanted to hear everything Gage knew about last night and I might just show him my chalkboard.

An hour later with full stomachs and fresh coffee in our cups, the conversation turned to the tragedy at the greenhouse.

Steve said, "I couldn't believe it when Nikki told me she and Lily found Dean Hartley dead." He shook his head. "Bad luck falling off the ladder like he did. I can't imagine needing help, being alone and seriously injured."

I watched Gage's face, which was always like an open book to me. How could I ask questions so that he'd actually answer me? Nikki was watching me closely and seemed to sense what I was thinking.

She turned her attention to Gage. "But was it an unfortunate accident? Last night you implied it could be something else, and Peabody and Mac basically confirmed it. And the way the ladder looked as if it had been placed near where Dean lay supports that theory. If he had fallen accidentally wouldn't it have been at an odd angle or he might have even been lying on top of it?"

Gage didn't look at Nikki, but instead studied me. "I can't comment on an ongoing investigation."

That was definitely for my benefit. I sat up straighter in the chair. "Then let's talk hypothetically."

Steve's mouth fell open as the gravity of the situation sank in. "Do you think the killer was still there when the girls arrived?"

Gage did a good job controlling his voice, but it cracked when he said, "There is no way to know for sure."

Steve clasped his hand over Nikki's. "You could have been next."

I heard the fear in his voice, and in an attempt to reassure him, I said, "Nikki and I can handle ourselves."

He knew that Nikki was a kitchen witch and I was in training, and reminding him of our abilities without coming right out and saying it seemed to allay his fears. Despite what Steve knew about us, I hadn't told Gage that I knew a limited amount of magic and had almost mastered a few spells that could help get me out of a difficult situation. Nikki's magic skills were finely honed compared to mine.

"Lily called me right after they found the body so even if the person who had been with Dean at the time of the incident was still there, they would have snuck off to avoid discovery."

Steve nodded but still looked pale. Milo stalked in and hopped up in his lap, pushing Steve's hand to the top of his head to pet him. I appreciated Milo trying to calm Steve. Was being empathic another one of his skills that I wasn't aware of, like reading?

"Okay, so let's get back to a possible scenario." I toyed with my coffee cup while I gathered my thoughts and thanked the stars Gage didn't rush me. He was either hoping I wouldn't pursue the topic, which of course we all knew that wasn't about to happen, or that I might have insight which could help him with the case.

Gage got up and grabbed the coffee pot and refilled everyone's cups. He glanced in the direction of the pantry. I couldn't help but smile. The man knew me so well. Without having to ask, he opened the door and slid the chalkboard out and set it up so we all had a clear view.

He studied my notes, and his brow quirked before saying, "You've been busy, Lily."

I gave a nonchalant shrug. "Jotting down some thoughts, just in case." I let that comment dangle since I loved puzzles, and murder was the biggest and most important puzzle I could solve.

He sat down and leaned forward. "Walk me through your process."

Finally, I had his undivided attention. "Dean argued with at least five individuals at some point yesterday, and then the grand finale was the argument with the entire garden club ganging up on him."

"And do you know if all the arguments were about the same thing?"

I gave an affirmative nod. "Roses. Well, except the one with Tucker. His was over hedge trimmers."

Nikki leaned back in her chair and gave a half laugh, half snort. "Who argues over flowers?"

"When there is money involved, people can argue about anything. And from what Dean told me while I was reading his tea leaves, roses are big money. Apparently, he announced the creation of a new hybrid rose at the festival. But some of the club members and others accused him of stealing it. I did some research last night, and roses are patented for at least twenty years to protect the growers who cultivate them. It takes a long time to develop a new hybrid so to make their money back, you just can't go and graft a new type as a new creation without breaking the law."

"Copyright infringement." Gage didn't say anything else while I was relaying what I had discovered.

Steve asked, "And Dean claimed to have created a new flower and the others said it was similar to someone else's?" Milo was still soaking up the attention from Steve like a sponge and based on his soothing tone of voice, my familiar was more relaxed now.

"My guess, similar but not identical." I picked up my coffee and took a sip. The warm brew hit the spot. "Of course, he was telling me some of this when he was sitting for his reading, so he blew it off like it was no big deal. Even though he was being accused of wrongdoing, it didn't faze him."

Nikki said, "Did you tell Gage about the tea leaves?"

"She did," he answered. "But I'm not sure I believe they can predict the future." With that verbal dismissal, I didn't go down that path again.

I picked up a scone and broke off a piece before placing the two halves on my plate. "We need to talk to these people and get their version of Dean's hybrid rose. Did he infringe on a patent or was it a huge misunderstanding?"

Gage said, "Lily, I need to talk to these people, not you. And what I'm about to say can't leave this room." He gave each one of us his stink eye and one by one we nodded.

"Based on the ladder, which Nikki pointed out, was placed away from Dean, this was not an accident."

He said as much to me last night. I opened my mouth to ask a question, but he held up his hand, and I snapped my mouth shut.

"What we don't have is a motive, and there is zero evidence to suggest who the perp might be. Dean didn't have any cameras on his property that we can find, but my investigators will be back out there today." He glanced at his watch. "And as much as I'd like to continue to enjoy another coffee in the company of good friends, I need to get out there too."

I stood and stacked the dirty dishes, my mind racing. Nikki and Steve got up to help, and I tossed a tiny piece of bacon to Milo who had jumped from Steve's lap and was now at my feet. He purred his thanks and trotted out of the room, his work done for now.

I wanted to go with Gage to the greenhouse; there might be something he'd overlook. Like that painted fingernail I had found. "Gage, can I..." My words fell away as he shook his head and gave me a stern look.

"Lily, you can't come to an active crime scene. I appreciate you want to help, and the research about the roses was very interesting. It's another thread for us to investigate, but you're not a police officer, and this is dangerous. There is a killer out there and most likely would kill again to protect their identity." He took my hand in his. "I know how you feel about jumping in with both feet. But do I need to remind you the last two times you got involved in a murder investigation, it put you in grave danger. I won't let that happen again."

How was I going to get him to see me as an asset, not as a problem? "It's okay. I'm going over to Aunt Mimi's this afternoon, but if you want to swing by later, we can catch up."

He narrowed his hazel eyes and cocked his head. "You won't go out to the crime scene?"

"I have a busy day. Stop over later if you want." I hoped sounding easy-breezy would convince him. And I didn't say I wasn't ever going out there, just that I was busy.

For the first time since he arrived, a warm and relaxed smile graced his mouth, and he pecked my cheek. "I'll see you later this afternoon."

Nikki gave me a sharp look, her brow arched. My agreeing to stay away had been far too easy, and she knew it. I couldn't risk answering her look with one of my own for now.

Gage slid the chalkboard back into the pantry as if out of sight would be out of mind, and if that gave him peace, I'd let him do it. It was just as easy to pull it back out again.

Once the table was cleared and the leftovers were in the kitchen, Gage's phone pinged. He looked at the incoming text. "I need to run, but I'll see you later." He shook Steve's hand, gave Nikki a friendly hug, and kissed my cheek again. "Say hi to your aunt for me."

Once the back door was closed and I heard his car start,

I leaned against the counter. "Nikki, are you up for a drive out to the greenhouse tomorrow morning?"

Steve shook his head. "Absolutely not. You ladies shouldn't go out there by yourselves. Whoever is responsible could be out there, waiting."

Nikki pecked his lips. "Stop. We don't have a serial killer on the loose, just someone who was really ticked at Dean and settled the argument in the worst way possible. Besides, you know we have special skills at our disposal. What could possibly go wrong?"

He smacked his head with the palm of his hand and groaned. "Lily, please don't drag Nikki into one of your bad ideas."

Before I could say a word, Nikki popped her hands on her hips. "Do you think letting Lily go out there by herself is a good idea? We're safer together, and I will not let my best friend go out there alone, so you can forget about it."

My heart swelled with gratitude. We had been friends for a long time, and she always had my back just as I did for her.

Steve looked from Nikki's determined face to mine, wearing the identical expression. "Then if the two of you are determined to go out there, I'm going with you."

I said, "You want to help us investigate?"

He grinned. "No. That isn't what I said. Consider me your unofficial bodyguard."

A light rap on the back door proceeded it being opened. Dax stuck his head in the door. "Lily, I'm sorry to barge in, but you have a large rosebush burning in your driveway."

"What?" I raced out the door and stopped a few feet away from a large ceramic pot of what had been a rosebush. I glanced over my shoulder. "Nikki. Steve. We're leaving at eight."

Chapter 5
Lily

The next morning, I dressed in jeans and a blouse under a heavy sweatshirt so I would be ready for work at the bookstore after Nikki, Steve, and I were done walking around the greenhouse looking for clues. I had called Gage about the burning rosebush and after he confirmed I was okay, he said he couldn't stop over until later in the day. The police officers must have taken much longer at the Hartley place than originally planned.

As I was waiting for the coffee to finish brewing, my cell rang. I answered it on speakerphone. "Hello."

"Good morning, Lily. It's Dax Peters." His deep voice held a hint of a deep Southern accent, but it was neutral of emotion. Like there was no smile on his face.

"Dax, this is a surprise." I forced a smile to my face since my plan was to ask him for coffee. I didn't want him to think I was cranky first thing in the morning or at any time.

"I'm surprised to find you home. I figured you would go out to Detective Erikson's crime scene."

Dang. This guy already knew me too well, and how did he know I was home? I crossed my fingers to keep from being jinxed as my slight fib rolled off my tongue. "I'm enjoying an extra dose of caffeine. Mondays are typically busy at the bookstore." That sounded hollow but with any luck he wouldn't figure out I was skirting the truth. It would be just like him to call Gage.

"I'm sure it is." He paused. "When I heard you had found the body, I... Well, I just wanted to make sure that you were alright. There can be a delayed shock from that kind of experience."

My heart sighed a little that he seemed to actually care about my feelings, and I was planning on using him to test my theory about dating. "Thanks. That's very kind of you, but I'm fine. The sight of blood has never bothered me. Maybe I should have been a doctor instead of a bookshop owner."

"I believe we all find our true calling if we listen to the universe." This time I heard the smile in his soft Southern drawl and was pleasantly surprised to know he believed what he was saying. I wasn't sure why I was so sure, but I just was.

"Like you becoming a detective?" I leaned against the counter and wondered if he'd answer the question.

"I like solving puzzles, we're alike that way. And every case I'm on is a labyrinth of twists and turns. It keeps my brain from becoming sluggish."

"I know exactly what you mean."

He chuckled. "That's why the recent crimes in Pembroke Cove have you captivated. All separate but inter-twined in some giant puzzle that you are dying to solve."

A chill raced down my spine as he said the word dying. That's when it hit me. Our small town has had three murders in four months, and I needed to ask Gage the statistics of how many murders usually happened in our neck of the woods. And then ask Aunt Mimi what could have caused the spike. Could something magical be at work?

Dax said, "The reason I called was to offer my assistance."

"Huh?" I was stunned with his last comment and could only stammer a one-word response.

He laughed again. "My case is at a standstill at the moment, and I have idle time on my hands. I have talked with Gage, and the current case doesn't seem to be related to my ongoing investigation. And despite what you've promised him, I know you will be poking around, and I'd bet you a cup of coffee that you are planning on taking a run out to the greenhouse today."

Should I say I'll take that bet, knowing I'll lose? It would be one way to have a get-together with him. Nope, I wasn't going to call it an official date; it's just to see if there was a romantic spark between us. Or I could just admit what I was planning and then ask him for coffee.

"Lily?" His deep voice reverberated in my ear. He did have a nice voice.

"Sorry, I was trying to decide if I should take you up on your bet."

"And?" he drawled in that oh-so-Southern way of his again that I did find utterly charming.

"You're on. If I start poking around at the greenhouse and you find out, then I'll meet you for coffee at the Copper Kettle. It's a charming coffee shop in town. In fact, if you prefer tea, the Copper Kettle stocks my mother's tea blends, and they're quite good."

"Isn't tea what got Dean Hartley into trouble?"

I wasn't sure if he was teasing or being serious. "He bought tea; he wasn't poisoned by it."

"In the police report, it said he had his tea leaves read prior to leaving the festival. Could it have been tainted or was it just the reading that might have put him off his game?"

This was curious. What did Dax know about tea leaves, and why would he ask me? But the even bigger question is, why would Gage have put that into the report? Was it relevant to the case? He had dismissed it as unimportant.

"Do you know anything about tea leaves?" My breath caught as I waited for Dax to respond.

"How about we save that answer for our coffee date."

That time I heard the teasing in his voice. We both knew I was going to look into the situation, so I made a snap decision. "If you'd like to meet me for coffee tomorrow, we can chat more about what I might or might not have seen in his cup." I left that dangling in the air, my heart quickening in my chest as I waited for him to answer.

"I have a better idea. Can you meet me at two this afternoon? We can have coffee, and you can tell me what you discovered this morning. That is if you can get away from your store."

A soft tap on the back door preceded it being opened. Nikki stuck her head in and winked when she saw I was on the phone. She was right on time.

I mouthed, *Can you cover the store for about an hour this afternoon?* She gave me a thumbs-up and grinned.

"I'll meet you at two, and whoever gets there first can grab a table."

"Better yet, I'll come by the bookstore, and we can walk over together. That way we'll get there at the same time." There was definitely a smile in his voice now.

"Sounds like a plan. I need to run, but I'll see you later."

"Say hi to Nikki and Steve for me."

The line clicked off as I said goodbye. That was odd. How did he know they were here? Then it dawned on me. He was here for the burning bush event and overheard when I said we were leaving at eight. And I walked right into the coffee get-together with his bet. I had been outmaneuvered, and I wasn't sure how I felt about that.

Nikki gave me a smile. "Was that Gage?"

I picked up my bag and keys. "No. Dax Peters. I'm going to meet him for coffee today, so thanks for covering the store."

A flash of confusion flitted over her face. "You're going on a date with Dax? But you're in love with Gage."

Nikki understood me. She always had, and that was just one of the reasons we were best friends. "Gage has never said he wanted to date me. We're just friends. He doesn't think about me any differently than Steve does. I want to go out and have fun with a guy. Dax seems like a nice man, so why not?"

"He's not Gage."

I wasn't going down that rabbit hole so early in the morning. I needed to table this conversation and focus on the larger issue, the murder of Dean Hartley. "We need to hurry if I'm going to open the store by ten."

About twenty minutes later, we arrived at the greenhouse, and our car was the only one in the parking area. With any luck, we'd be in and out fast.

I looked at Nikki in the passenger seat and glanced over my shoulder at Steve. "Here's the plan. Take pictures of everything. We can review them later for anything we might miss while we're here. Even if we take duplicate shots of the same thing, an angle might be slightly different."

They both nodded and Nikki swallowed hard. "Are you sure we'll be safe?"

I scanned the area, and other than the leaves rustling softly in the morning breeze, we were alone. "I'm sure, but let's stick close together." I saw a flash of panic in Nikki's eyes. "I've never cast the protection spell that would move as we wandered around so as a precaution, you need to remember something very important." I squeezed her hand and said, "We have skills most people don't." And for dramatic effect, I jerked my thumb over my shoulder. "And your fiancé is with us so if magic fails, we've got brawn."

She visibly relaxed. "You're right, and I know you've been practicing your spells, but we've never worked our magic together. Would it be strong enough if we needed it?"

Nikki brought up a good point. We had never tried to cast a spell at the same time. What if we overpowered the other? Was that even possible? Pushing that thought aside, I said, "Are you kidding? We'd kick magical butt and wouldn't need to take names." I grinned. "Ready?"

With a quick nod, she pushed open her door, and Steve unfolded his tall, lanky frame from the back seat. "We should have taken my truck. It's more comfortable for three people."

I wrinkled my nose. "It's much harder to hide a truck than my Mini Cooper should the need arise."

He shook his head. "I'm not sure I like how your mind works." He kissed Nikki's cheek. "I know she's your best friend and all, but she's a little nutty."

Nikki laughed. "I know and isn't it great?"

To keep the couple from going down the path of how crazy I was, I held up my cell phone with the flashlight app blazing. "Ready?"

They did the same and without talking, we walked

around the right side of the greenhouse. I made a mental note that we'd need to come back the opposite way since the killer might have done the same.

As we scanned the area in a grid pattern like blood-hounds, we took pictures of every blade of grass and possible clue while birds chirped overhead. The sun was finally making her appearance over the tall trees, and it promised to be a beautiful fall day. So far, I hadn't found anything that I'd consider a decent clue. The bright-yellow crime scene tape fluttered in the cool breeze.

I said, "Don't go into the actual scene. Just in case the police officers haven't finished processing it, we won't want to contaminate it." Not that either of them needed to be reminded to be careful, but I felt better saying something. It was eerily quiet and getting on my nerves.

We continued to make our way around the side of the grassy area when Nikki stopped. "Lily, come here."

I jogged around the back side, and Steve joined us too. She was taking a picture of something at the border of the tree line about twenty feet from the edge of the crime scene tape.

She said, "I would have overlooked it, but the sun glinted off the metal." As she leaned over to pick up a USB drive, I grabbed her arm to stop her.

"Wait. It might have fingerprints on it." I withdrew a plastic sandwich bag from my front jeans pocket. "Use this, and then we can turn it inside out and protect the drive. But first we need to take pictures of where we found it, how it looked. Gage always has Sharon or Mac do that so we need to do the same." If Nikki and Steve were thinking we should let Gage know what we had found, they never said a word.

After I was done with my documentation, Steve said, "I'll pick it up." He held up the bag before handing me the

USB drive. "Are you going to turn it over to the police when we get back to town?"

I frowned. "I'd rather have a look at what's on it first. It could be Dean's. There is no way to know how long it's been there either. Maybe one of the police officers dropped it."

I knew that was a stretch since it didn't have any frost on it, but the last thing we needed was for anyone to get worried we had tampered with evidence. Which we kind of had since we were taking it from the crime scene. Maybe after I looked at what was on the drive, I could put it back where we found it and no one would be the wiser, including Gage.

My cell phone rang, and it was Dax. Right after I said hello, he said, "Just a heads-up. I saw a cruiser and Gage's car driving out of town. As an educated guess, they're headed out to the Hartley placc."

Dang it. "Thanks." I stuck the phone in my pocket and said, "We need to go. Company is on the way."

Steve slipped the plastic bag in his shirt pocket, and we hurried around the opposite side of the greenhouse in the direction of the car. I drew up short. Standing between us and our escape was a very large dog. A low warning growl emanated from deep inside him.

My voice was strangled as I attempted to joke, "Does anyone speak dog?"

Nikki touched my hand and whispered, "Stay put." She took a step forward and kept her eyes on the dog. My heart rate kicked into high gear when I imagined her getting attacked by the oversized fur ball.

Steve leaned close to me and whispered, "She's got this, don't worry. Remember her familiar is a dog."

Nikki inched closer to the animal, all the while saying

something only the dog could hear. Since its ears twitched, I longed to exhale, but it still hadn't backed down its aggressive posture. But Nikki didn't seem to be afraid, and I was impressed. If that had been me, I would have left the car and started walking back to town.

I glanced at my watch. Ten minutes had elapsed since Dax's call, and Gage would be here soon. We needed to hurry. Nikki had stretched out her hand, and even though I told Dax blood didn't bother me, there was no way I wanted to see Nikki's today.

My breath hitched, and Steve put a comforting hand on my arm. "Shh." That was all he needed to say to keep me glued to his side in silence.

The dog's body posture was softening, and the growling had stopped. It was working. Nikki was making a new four-legged friend. A minute later, which seemed like an hour, she was scratching the dog's head and behind his ears. She twirled the collar around his neck and called over her shoulder, "His name is Brutus, and he belongs to Dean. I'll bet he's scared and hungry, but how did everyone overlook him? He should have been taken to the shelter in town."

I said, "Will he let us get into the car? We need to go."

Nikki turned away from us and continued to pet the dog. "I'm not leaving him."

I looked between Nikki, Steve, the dog, and my very small car.

Steve grinned. "See, we should have brought the truck."

We didn't have time to joke about that now, so without responding to him, I said, "Come on. We'll make it work, but time is running out. If Gage finds us here, he's going to be ticked."

"Come on, Brutus. You're going for a ride in Lily's car." She opened up the driver's door and folded the seat forward. "Hop in, baby." He did as she asked like they had been a bonded pair forever instead of mere minutes.

Steve grumbled. "I'd better have enough leg room so I don't get a cramp."

Nikki glared at him. "We are not leaving him behind, so deal with it."

I had never heard that iron tone in her voice with Steve or anyone before. He must have known that was her *don't mess with me* voice, and he got in the passenger side. I slid behind the wheel.

My intuition was tingling. Gage was close, and we needed to get out of sight. I started the car and went in the opposite direction from town. I remembered an old farm stand a short way down the road. We could wait there for a while until everyone had parked and walked behind the greenhouse.

"Where are we going?" Nikki asked.

"We're going to hide for a bit and then head for town." The old stand hid my small car perfectly. I smirked in the rearview mirror and caught Steve's eye. "Good idea?"

He grinned. "Yeah, my truck would stick out like a lighthouse at night."

I nodded and checked the time. I'd give it fifteen minutes, then we'd head back to town, and hopefully, Gage would be none the wiser.

Chapter 6
Gage

The moment I stepped out of the car, I scanned the area. It felt like I was being watched. Shaking off the feeling, I looked around the parking area and even the wooded part near the road and was a little surprised to not see Lily's car. Maybe she wasn't going to start poking around this homicide. I snorted and reminded myself of who I was thinking about. That woman loved a challenge, and what was going on in town with this string of violent crimes was far too tempting. Pembroke Cove was a sweet little New England seaside town, and the worst that typically happened was an occasional fight at the local waterfront bar. I adjusted my shoulder harness, keeping my sidearm close. I couldn't shake the feeling something wasn't quite right here.

Peabody and Mac had already fanned out, walking in a grid pattern to see if the crime scene investigators from Portland had missed anything. They were trained to be thorough, but fresh eyes were critical, and my people knew this town better. It was that simple.

I unlocked the greenhouse and entered the garden tool area off the back through the open overhead door and noticed a variety of tools hanging on the wall. Everything seemed to have its place, and the workbench was neat and tidy. I scanned the tools again. And there it was, not a single space was open as if a tool, like pruners, had been taken from the wall. In fact, there were two pairs of pruners hanging farther down, close to the back door. *If Hartley had two sets in here and it seemed if all the tools were in place, where did the new shears come from?* I made a note to take a closer look at the loppers in the evidence room.

I stepped back into the crisp morning air, looking to see where Peabody and Mac were. They were close to the wood line, about twenty feet from the yellow tape. Peabody was squatting, and Mac was taking a picture.

Closing the distance between us, I called out, "What did you find?"

Peabody held up an empty plastic sandwich bag with the tip of her pen. "It looks new, and I'm certain it wasn't here before this morning."

"Why do you say that?" I drew close and surveyed the area.

"We had a heavy frost last night, and this is dry."

I nodded and turned in a circle. It was then I noticed footprints in the frosted grass. They were faint, but definitely someone had been out here. Was that connected to the baggie? "Have you found anything else?"

Mac said, "Nothing. We still need to check the immediate perimeter where the body was discovered."

I didn't need to acknowledge his comment. Instead, I followed the trail of fast-evaporating prints around the greenhouse to the gravel parking area. Of course, they ended at the edge of the grass, but there were three sets. If it had been two, I would have concluded it was Lily and Nikki, but who could be the third? Who would have agreed to come out there? Not everyone was into poking around a crime scene, and that's when it hit me. Steve.

He had sent me a text last night, and I never responded. I pulled out my cell to read it again. *Don't worry. The burning bush was a minor thing. Lily is safe, and I intend to keep both ladies that way.*

I'd bet my last twenty bucks that Steve came out here this morning to make sure nothing happened to Lily or Nikki. But how long had they been here, when had they left, and why? Had they found something, and if they had, why hadn't Lily called me? Were they the ones to drop the plastic bag? I had too many questions and zero answers.

"Guys." Mac and Peabody stopped what they were doing and waited. Even with the short time of working together in this capacity, they understood me. "I need to go into town. Can you carry on?"

Mac looked at Peabody and with a glint in his eye, he said, "I'm not sure, but somehow we'll handle the job."

A rare grin graced Peabody's face. "We'll muddle through." Then she winked at me. "Going to chat with your favorite amateur sleuth?"

"Yes. I think she beat us out here this morning and she had two accomplices."

Mac nodded. "She was smart not to come alone. It's desolate out here."

Which made it the perfect crime scene. "I'll catch you at the station, and take your time. There still might be some-thing that we missed."

. . .

When I got back to town, I didn't go right to the bookstore but made a stop at the police station. I wanted to check out the hedge pruners to see if there was anything to discover. Once in my office, I grabbed latex gloves and swiped my badge to gain access to the evidence room. Everything was in alphabetical order by victim's last name, something Peabody had instituted when she arrived, and it made perfect sense. I couldn't understand why we hadn't done it before. I easily located the oversized tub and placed it on the table.

Withdrawing the pruners, it was easy to see they were brand new and the price tag bore a distinctive logo—Tuckers Hardware. For the first time, we had just caught a lucky break. Now to see who might have purchased this item in the last two weeks. If it was Hartley himself, that wouldn't be any help at all. I turned them over in my hands and noticed the hefty weight of them. It wouldn't have been easy to handle them with just one hand. Someone used them with intent. I wished I could believe it was a terrible accident and someone had been too scared to call for help. To abandon him while he was bleeding to death was a crime. I stowed the box and tossed the gloves in the garbage. Next stop, The Cozy Nook Bookshop.

It was late morning by the time I left the police station after being waylaid with another case. I arrived at the bookstore, and Lily was standing in the front window when I parked. I hesitated. Should I grab coffee for us or stop in empty-handed? I usually brought her something from the Sweet Spot Bakery. Before I could make up my mind, she saw me, her smile lighting up her face as she waved me in.

Before I could open the door, she had. "Hello there."

She closed it after I walked in. "Just in time for coffee. I could use a pick-me-up."

I glanced around the store and saw everything was neat and tidy as usual. Milo came skulking out from the small kitchen area. He paused before heading in my direction, snaking around my legs and purring. I bent over and scooped him up.

Lily laughed softly. "He has a soft spot for you."

I scratched between the cat's ears and grinned. "It goes both ways."

She moved in the direction of the coffee pot. "I picked up some muffins at the Sweet Spot before I opened the store today. They're pumpkin. William was out of pecan cinnamon buns but promised to save me a couple tomorrow." She looked over her shoulder and gave me the smile that always kicked my heart into a rapid staccato.

"I'm sure he hated to disappoint you. After all, he knows they're your favorite."

With a soft laugh, Lily fixed two mugs with cream and sugar while the coffee brewed. "It should be just another minute." She looked turned and asked, "Busy morning?"

"The usual kind." That little minx, she had been up to something earlier. I could feel it in my bones. "And you, many customers?"

"The days can either be busy or quiet."

That was a noncommittal answer too. Both of us were dancing around with vague words and no direct looks.

Someone needed to break this tightrope we were on. "I was out at the Hartley place this morning."

Her brow shot to her hairline, but casually, she said, "Really? Everything alright out there?" She handed me the first mug of coffee and avoided looking directly in my eyes while she started to pour the next cup. "It's not like anything else can happen. Dean lived alone."

I nodded and wondered where she was going with this.

She said, "As far as I know, he never got married and didn't have any kids. He seemed to be alone in the world." Lily's face softened while she looked at Milo. "Do you think he had a pet? I know how much Milo means to me. I talk to him all the time."

Milo headbutted my chin, and I placed him on the floor. "When we searched the house, we didn't see any evidence of a cat." Which was a tiny misdirection of the truth, since we had discovered large dog bones, a huge bowl, and a bag of kibble, but Lily was hiding something.

"What about a dog? A person lives that far out of town, gardens all day, and he doesn't have a pet. Don't you think that's odd?"

"I guess you think it is?" I waited for Lily to cross the room to the wingback chairs that sat near the front of the store. They were reading chairs for customers, but we often enjoyed coffee and a pastry while we discussed books, movies, and more recently, murder.

"What if," she drawled out, "he had a dog. What would happen to it now?"

Just as I suspected, she knew about Brutus. "At this point in our investigation, if we had found a pet and there was no one who came forward to care of it, we'd take it to the shelter until more permanent arrangements could be found."

Her hand flew to her mouth. "Like put him to..." She shuddered and before she said the word, I jumped in.

"No." The word came out more like a bark. "Absolutely not. He'll get adopted." Dang it, that all but confirmed there was a dog, even though I hadn't found him yet.

A triumphant grin filled her face. "Good to know."

I tipped my chin down and lifted my eyes in her direction. "Lily. What do you think you know?"

Her eyes met mine, and this time there was a hint of a challenge lingering there. "There's a Brutus."

I sat up straight in the chair and scanned the room. Not that she could hide a large dog anywhere in the shop. "Do you have the dog?"

She sipped her coffee and shrugged, making me wait. "I don't."

"But you know who does. Lily, stop playing games. A dog's life is important too."

With a wrinkle of her nose, she said, "I know that, but I needed to make sure no harm would come to the big baby."

"You know me. I'd never let that happen. Now where is he?"

"With Nikki. We found him, and his collar had a tag with his name and owner's information. Since he was alone in the world, it was an easy decision to take care of the dog until other—friendly—arrangements can be made. Like an adoption."

"He wasn't injured?"

She furrowed her brow. "Other than being hungry and thirsty, he was fine. I mean, considering he'd been wandering outside since Saturday."

I nodded. If the dog had been around when the incident happened and it was intentional, wouldn't the dog have tried to protect Dean?

"Brutus wasn't injured in any way so I'm going to surmise he wasn't present during the altercation."

I sagged into the chair. Why did she have to do that, always know what I was thinking? "If he was in the house, how did he get out? If he was outside, why didn't he try to defend Dean? Does this mean Brutus knew the person and didn't feel threatened?"

"Slow down, Detective. Rapid-fire questions aren't the way to figure this out." Lily handed me a muffin. "Eat something and let's take this one question at a time."

I bit into the muffin and savored the spicy moist cake. William did have a way with baked goods. "You were at the scene this morning." I didn't bother to phrase it as a question. It was a forgone conclusion at this point.

She nodded. "Before you get all worried after the fact, I was with Nikki and Steve. Safety in numbers."

At least that assuaged one fear of mine.

"We decided to take another look after Dax discovered the rosebush burning in my driveway. It was obvious someone was trying to get my attention. Now I'm wondering if it wasn't to solve the mystery, but instead to find the dog."

I snorted a laugh. "You think the murderer has a heart?"

Her lips formed a frown. "At least for something with four legs—two, maybe not so much. And it was a good thing we went out there. Nikki did a great job coaxing the frightened dog into the car."

With a double take, I laughed. "Wait, did you fit three adults and a dog that is as large as a person in your little car?" The laugh rolled up from my toes and soon my entire body was shaking from a deep belly laugh.

"Well, taking Steve's truck was too much vehicle," she said with a sniff. "It's not that funny, and what would you have done? Leave the poor dog to fend for itself?"

"Of course not. But why didn't you just call the town hall and ask the animal control officer to go out and pick up the dog?"

She looked out the window as if the people on the sidewalk were the most interesting part of her day.

"Are you going to tell me what else you found at the crime scene, other than a one-hundred-pound dog?" Lily's eyes grew wide, and I had her. There was more to this morning's escapade other than the dog.

Chapter 7
Lily

I fidgeted in my chair. Darn Gage for jumping to the conclusion that I discovered more than Brutus at the Hartley place. The USB drive was stashed at the bottom of my bag, still in the plastic baggie Steve used to pick it up.

"What makes you think I—or should I say we—found anything?" I used my best haughty tone of voice with the hope that it would make him feel bad. I snuck a look at him from the corner of my eye to discover he was watching me intently. There was no facial expression at all, and it was inevitable I would be the one to crack first. However, I wasn't about to cave too quickly. He needed to stew a bit.

"What did you find when you were at the scene of the crime?" I asked.

"Three sets of footprints in the frost-covered grass. If we had gone out later in the morning, the sun would have caused them to evaporate." He sipped his coffee, playing his waiting game.

I stifled a laugh behind my hand. At least now I knew how he discovered it might have been me. Thankfully, he hadn't seen my car as I pulled from the hiding spot at the old farm stand.

He quirked an eyebrow. "Is something amusing?"

I shook my head. "Not at all. I was thinking how lucky you were that Mother Nature helped with your investigation."

A slip of a smile appeared on Gage's lips and hovered for a microsecond before fading away. "Are you ready to tell me what you found? I'm going to hazard a guess that it was something near the tree line."

It was time to give in. I threw up my hands and then clapped them together. "For the record, we did not go inside the taped-off area. All we did was look. But you're right. As we were leaving, Brutus was waiting next to the car and Nikki made friends with him. We couldn't leave him out there with no water or food."

"You said that the dog is at Nikki's."

"She will foster him until someone wants to adopt him. She thought he had been through enough and being stuck in a shelter would upset the pup even more."

"And what about Murphy?" he asked.

I was surprised he thought to ask about Nikki's golden retriever. "Murphy's easygoing, and making new friends is a snap. Nikki thought it would be good for both dogs to have some companionship." I stopped short of telling Gage that after a short conversation with Murphy, explaining the situation, he'd be fine with fostering the now family-less dog. But that would entail revealing the witch and familiar connections, and I was not ready for that.

His eyes narrowed, and he leaned forward, forearms resting on his thighs. "What else did you find? It's time to fess up. It could be important to the case so you must tell me."

All my diversions didn't stop him from pressing me for the truth. It wasn't like I had planned to never tell him, but I wanted to see what was on the drive first. My shoulders slumped. "There was a USB drive almost obscured in the undergrowth just at the tree line. We wouldn't have seen it if the sun hadn't hit it just right. It was like we were meant to find it." The minute the words were out of my mouth, I knew that was a dumb excuse.

"Lily. You can't just remove evidence from the scene of a crime."

I held up my hand. "In my defense, I know it wasn't there at the time of the murder."

He shook his head. "And how do you know that?"

"It was dry."

Gage's face scrunched up, clearly confused. "Ah. No frost?"

I had to give him the USB drive and convince him to let me open it before he took it to the station. "It wasn't damp from the frost. Therefore, someone had dropped it even more recent, like before we arrived."

Hurrying from the room, I retrieved the baggie from my purse and grabbed my laptop on the way back to where Gage was still waiting for me.

Holding it in the air, I said, "I'll give this to you, but I need a favor first."

A frown appeared on his mouth, and the creases in his forehead deepened. "I'm afraid to ask."

"Let me look at the files before you take it."

He began to shake his head, and it looked like it was about to pop off. "Gage. You might not have found this if it weren't for me, Nikki, and Steve. The least you can do is let me have a little peek, please?"

He held out his hand, palm flat. He didn't have to say a

word. I knew that look and it wasn't a happy one. "You didn't touch it, did you?"

"No. We were very careful and picked it up with the bag." Reluctantly, I placed the baggie in his hand. Then he withdrew a pair of latex gloves from his jacket pocket and put them on. "Fire up your laptop. You can't open it, but I can. And for your sake, I hope there's not a virus on the drive."

I did as he asked and chewed on the corner of my bottom lip. I hadn't thought about a virus. Searching my memory, I wondered if there was a spell for protecting my computer, but nothing sprang to mind. I wished Milo would skulk around like he usually did and he could tell me if there was a spell in *Practical Beginnings* which covered electronics. But it didn't matter. Gage was clicking icons, and within seconds, whatever was on the drive would be on the screen.

There was an unlabeled manila folder icon on the USB. Just one. I looked at Gage as he looked at me. He asked, "Ready?"

Rubbing my hands together with anticipation, I nodded. Even if there was a virus, I had that protection software installed so hopefully nothing would crash my system. I leaned forward to get a closer look and his familiar, woodsy cologne wrapped around me. I gave him a surreptitious look before refocusing on the screen.

Gage double-clicked the folder icon, and instantly ten more icons came up. All pictures since they had a dot jpg extension. My finger itched to reach over and start clicking, but I held back. Gage was kind enough to let me look, so I needed to be patient.

"What do you think we'll see?" he asked.

"With any luck, there will be a selfie of the perp." I

lifted my eyes to meet his and could see the glint of a laugh hovering in them. "What, you don't think it's possible?"

"Highly unlikely since you'd have to transfer the pictures from the device that took them to this USB. If there was a selfie, it would be deleted."

I pointed to the laptop. "Let's see what's on here."

The images began to load, and at first, I was confused. Image after image were of roses in various stages of growth, and then there was a shot of Dean hunched over a potting bench, so intent he seemed oblivious to whoever was taking the pictures or even if he had known he was being photographed.

"These could be a couple of years old."

Gage opened the image files and then clicked on the magnifying glass. He zeroed in on a calendar, and we could see it was from earlier in the year. Well, that shot that theory down the drain.

He said, "Whoever took these must have done it on the sly. Look at the angle. Nothing is overly direct. I wonder if they used a hidden camera."

"Who would hide a camera in a greenhouse?"

"Lily, I've been researching the business of roses, and new hybrids can be worth megabucks. If someone thought Dean was onto a big payday, they could want a cut of the action."

"Or cut him out entirely. Better still, if they thought he was doing something underhanded, that could also be motive for the cameras as proof of any allegations." I peered closer. "But there doesn't seem to be anything here that indicates who the person behind the camera is." My voice trailed off. I turned away from the screen to look at Gage. "What if this was a security camera that Dean installed and someone got ahold of the footage and pulled images from it."

He looked at me and grinned. "Great idea. You may have just found another piece of the puzzle."

"Maybe not the actual piece, but we know there is a missing connection to the security footage." I was proud that I could help Gage find threads to tug. "We need to go out to the greenhouse and see if we can locate more cameras, and I'll bet the digital recording unit is in his house."

"I'll call Mac to see if he can stop at the house and take a look while we head to the greenhouse." He logged into the police department server and saved the folder and then sent himself an email with the link to them. Before he withdrew the USB drive, he pushed the laptop my way.

"Care to shut down your system?" He wiggled his eyebrows. Was he suggesting I'd save the files before I gave him the drive? Not that he could come right out and say it since that would be a violation of something to do with chain of evidence, I was sure. If I had gotten to it first, that's what I would have done. And then turn the drive over to Gage for closer inspection.

"It will only take a minute." With my fingers flying over the keyboard, a copy of the folder now sat on my computer's desktop. I took the glove he handed to me and withdrew the small, slim device and handed it to him before I shut the laptop cover. I gave him a smile of thanks, and he returned with a half nod. It was all so clandestine it was almost comical.

I looked at my watch. "I can close the store for lunch, but any idea how long we'll be gone?"

He chuckled. "Why, do you have a date?"

I swallowed hard. This was not how I wanted Gage to

find out I was having coffee with Dax or if I even wanted him to know. "I. Um. Have an appointment at two. Do you think we'll be back to town by then?"

The smile, which had graced his face, faded, and he seemed to lose his spark. I felt bad. I should have called it a date since by the look on his face he already guessed the truth. "We should take two cars." That was the best way to make sure I was back in time for coffee, and I wasn't about to stand Dax up.

"Sure." Gage's voice was flat, and he averted his eyes. Did I see a flash of disappointment in them? I couldn't be sure. But I was not about to apologize for meeting a nice, handsome man for a simple coffee.

"I'll tell Milo we're leaving."

Without waiting for me, Gage strode to the door. He turned with his hand on the doorknob, his face devoid of all expression. "I'll see you out there, and remember you're a civilian accompanying me at my request and any information we find is confidential."

"I know. You don't need to remind me." Instantly, I regretted the snappish words. Sometimes this man irritated me to no end. He walked out and closed the door with a firm thud.

"Well, that was interesting." Milo's familiar grumble made me spin around.

"I don't know why he's so upset."

Milo stalked across the room and hopped up on the sales counter. He sat down, and with the tip of his head sideways, he gave me a curious look. "Think about it." He got up and stretched before jumping to the floor with a soft thud. He jogged across the room and settled in the window seat on a small fluffy blanket I had left for him.

"What's that supposed to mean?"

Milo lifted his head and gave me a sharp look. "You guys are like peanut butter and jelly, popcorn and butter, peas in a pod."

I crossed my arms over my chest and frowned. "We're not a couple."

"Apparently, the only two who don't know that are you and Gage. And you'd better decide if you want him to stay in your life. If you do, tell him how you feel." He stretched out as long as he could make his body and turned to face the window.

I stamped my foot with a thud. "You're exasperating. Tell me what to do."

"Lily, I'm your familiar to guide you in all things magical. That does not extend to your love life. For that you have Nikki, your mother, or Aunt Mimi."

"That's why I agreed to have coffee with Dax." I wanted to get Milo's full attention. "Milo!"

"Which brings me to another topic." He sat up and began to rub his paw over his face before finally saying, "When was the last time you practiced a new spell? From what I've seen, you haven't even opened *Practical Beginnings* since last week when you wanted to learn about reading tea leaves."

Why did he always revert every conversation to reading the book? "I had to look authentic with my readings." It was meant to come out as words of protest, but as I spoke, I realized the significance of my comment. "Milo." I rushed forward to sit down next to him. "The book never has shown me what I didn't need to know. Each spell that has appeared on the pages, out of sequence from what Aunt Mimi has said, it's because I needed to know it. Right?"

His green eyes flickered with approval. "Yes, every time. The book is guiding you and sadly, you're not giving it enough time on a regular basis. You treat it like it's an occasional thing to open and peruse, but to develop your craft, it takes careful and focused study. Even now it's sitting in your tote bag, waiting to be opened and read."

"You make it sound like it's alive." I glanced at the bag sitting on the floor at the side of the counter. "Is it?" My heart rate kicked up, thinking that I was overlooking something important.

"Of course not," Milo growled in his low kitty tone. "But it is magical, and you need to respect it."

My shoulders slumped at his direct, but gentle admonishment. I wasn't honing my skills by letting myself get distracted by a new murder and having coffee with Dax. I had some hard thinking to do, but first I needed to get out to the greenhouse, then have coffee and make sure Dax knew we were just friends and nothing romantic would blossom between us. And then there was Gage. I finally had come to a decision; I was going to be brave and tell him how I felt about him. Even if he didn't return those same feelings, I needed to be honest. Finally, Milo had made another good point. I needed to dedicate consistent time and focus to learning more about what the book contained. I was a witch, and it was high time I embraced it.

I scooped Milo up and hugged him tight to my chest while he squirmed and batted my cheek with his paw. "Thank you, my friend. You might not think you have good advice for all things that have to do with my life, but your words give me clarity." I kissed his soft head and placed him back on the cushion. "Keep an eye on things while I'm gone. I'm taking an extended lunch."

I heard him scold me as I closed the door. "Maybe you should tell Detective Cutie the truth before you have your coffee date."

Chapter 8
Lily

I t took me twenty minutes to reach Dean's place, and Gage's black police issued sedan was parked close to the greenhouse. I parked next to his car. I locked my handbag inside and looked around. Gage was nowhere to be seen, and the woods seemed to creep closer to the greenhouse each time I came out here. It was a fanciful notion, as if the trees knew Dean was gone and they could reclaim the land.

I shook off the oppressive thoughts and hurried to the side door of the greenhouse. Pushing it open, I realized I was alone in the space. Without Gage there, I could immerse myself in the room and attempt to figure out why anyone would want him dead.

The warm air enveloped me like a cloak and reminded me of summer, with its warm earthy smell like a garden having been tilled recently. I noticed a digital thermometer on the wall that read eighty. That explained the summerlike temps. The space was huge with rows and rows of roses. Some were small cuttings with plastic bags secured over them. Others had buds while others were in bloom. Overhead lighting dangled from wires over all the tables. With this setup, he must have been able to sell roses to florists. I guessed his business was much more extensive than selling at the farmer's markets and other events around town.

Now I studied the layout of the greenhouse. Besides the long rows of wooden benches with LED grow lights strung everywhere, on the back wall was Dean's potting bench with a solitary stool. At least in the pictures Gage and I had seen, that is what he was doing there. Next to that was a sturdy metal shelf unit with rows of bottles, and some had bright-colored labels—red, yellow, green, and blue. From this distance, it was easy to tell whatever those contents were could be hazardous to one's health. Overall, the space had the air of someone who had been hard at work but well organized. I thought about Dean's booth at the festival, and the two spaces had a cohesive look. This was his domain, and he had worked alone.

I walked to the end of one row and saw stacks of thick cardboard boxes that could be used for packing and shipping delicate blooms. It seemed to make sense to have this type of operation in Maine so flowers didn't have to travel as far in the winter months.

There was so much I hadn't considered when it came to flowers and a commercial operation. Would he have risked it all for some quick cash by ripping off someone else's patent? As I drew closer to the workbench, I saw stacks of three-ring binders. Each one had a numerical notation on the edge, but it wasn't a date. I picked up the one closest to me and flipped it open, scanning the first two pages. This contained dates, measurements, soil conditions, amounts of water, fertilizer, and even stages of the plant all listed in neat penmanship. I made my way through the rest of the book. I surmised this was all related to one specific plant as the number on the spine was reiterated repeatedly.

I pulled the next binder from the bench, and it was very similar but with a different code. Dean was conducting experiments on plants. Maybe he *had* stolen someone's rose and was trying to graft it, but without knowing the specifics of that hybrid and rootstock, it wasn't as easy as taking a cutting and grafting it.

The side door banged, and Gage strode in. "Lily. I didn't know you had arrived. I was just walking around the building, trying to figure out how the person who stabbed Dean could sneak up on him. You should have found me before you came in here." He closed the door. "I'm not sure what's going to happen to these plants. I plan to talk with Alvin Springs. He might know how to care for them from his garden club connections until we know what Dean's family wants to do."

I leaned into a stunning pink rose bloom and inhaled the sweet fragrant scent. "He was talented. All the plants should be in a magazine spread for roses." I met his eyes as he watched me. It was odd to see his eyes filled with sadness before he looked away.

"Have you found any cameras yet?"

I lifted my shoulders and tipped my head. "I haven't started to look." I gestured to the binders. "I found these. It looks as if he was tracking plants' progress. Nothing I can say specifically to any one plant since each one is referenced by a code. But I think the rumors could be right; he might have been involved in something illegal."

With a frown, Gage moved to the bench where I had left the binders open. "You're jumping to a conclusion based on what you saw at the festival. Where is the evidence?"

"It's in there. If he wasn't doing something illegal, why didn't he just spell out what flower was what hybrid, instead of this smoke and mirror data gathering?"

"Dean is not the first man to avoid specifics. I would do the same thing if I were the kind of guy who was experimenting with something. And think about what you see in the movies; all scientists use some sort of tracking system. Maybe he didn't want anyone to steal his new hybrid."

I tossed him a haphazard smile. "You could be right, and for the record, I know you don't experiment. You just plow ahead and get things done. No trial and error for you. Thinking on your feet is your style."

"Good to know you've noticed." His slow and easy grin appeared, pushing away the sadness that had been in his eyes moments earlier.

"You've always been that way, but it isn't necessarily the best way to get the desired end result. Sometimes thinking about a problem for longer than ten seconds yields a better outcome." I tipped back my head and scanned the wall about eight feet from the floor and along the ceiling, looking for places cameras could be hidden, but I was surprised to see them in plain view. "Look. Dean had to have installed the security cameras. But how did someone get copies of the pictures on the USB drive I found, and what had they discovered? Was it the reason Dean was killed?"

Grabbing a stepladder from beside the metal shelf, he took a long look at the camera closest to the workbench. "This is pretty sophisticated. It's hardwired, and once we find the receiver, we should be able to narrow down our suspects."

I scanned the room and walked to the back door, looking across the grass between where I stood and where I had discovered Dean a few days earlier. "That's only going to help if he had rigged cameras outside too. If the person who did this never came inside, we're back to square one."

Gage gave her a sharp look. "We don't have anything. But I might."

Groaning, I whirled around. "Why do you insist on putting up a roadblock now? If it wasn't for me, you wouldn't have the USB drive. I found it and Brutus. You didn't even know where the dog was."

He was nodding, and I knew he would find it hard to keep me at arm's length now. I had pointed out that I was an obvious asset to this operation. Not that I was equipped in the same way he was, but I had talent and a different set of skills.

"You're right, you did both of those things. But this is police business, and you should remember when you were involved, you were almost killed not once, but twice."

I sniffed. "That is a matter of interpretation. And for the record, I had both of those situations completely under control."

He snorted a laugh this time. "Good to know." His cell chirped with an incoming text message. He glanced at the screen and said, "It's Mac. I need to call him." Gage dialed the phone and walked out the door, closing it firmly behind him.

So much for me getting to listen to the one-sided conversation. I slowly made a trip around the perimeter of the greenhouse and took a closer look at the shelf with the bottles and boxes. As I was perusing them, I wasn't surprised to see how many items stated, *Do Not Ingest* or *Seek Medical Attention*. There were soda bottles, all unlabeled, holding amounts of various liquids, and it made me wonder if any of those contained deadly substances. Before

I could mull that over for too long, the back door burst open. Gage leaned inside.

"I need to go to Hartley's house. But I'll call you later."

I took a couple of steps in his direction. "I'll come with you."

His face blank, he held up his left arm and tapped the face of his watch. "Don't you have someplace to be?"

Inwardly, I groaned. Would it be in poor taste to cancel coffee with Dax this late? My mom and Aunt Mimi would have my hide if I did something so rude without a very good reason, and I don't think tagging along with Gage would qualify. I held back on my impulse based on years of being taught manners when I gave him a smile. "Dinner tonight at my place. I'll cook something simple, and we can talk about the case."

His eyes narrowed. "Are you sure your date will be happy if you have dinner with me?"

What the heck? Without thinking, I blurted out, "Meeting a new friend for coffee isn't a big deal. I can have breakfast, lunch, dinner, or coffee with whomever I'd like." My tone was sharp and I didn't care. "It's just coffee. Nothing more."

"Dax might not have the same point of view."

His simple statement caused my mouth to hang open. "How did you know I was meeting him?"

"I'm a detective, remember?" His tone sounded half-teasing, but it didn't match the look of regret in his eyes. "Besides, I didn't know for sure until you confirmed it."

Sputtering, I said, "But I didn't confirm anything."

His body seemed to sag under the weight of my words. "You just did."

I wanted to protest that it really wasn't that big of a deal, but then I drew up short. Why did I need to defend my decision to go on a simple date? Gage was acting as if I had just betrayed him with the enemy. "So, do you want to come over for dinner and talk about all of this?" I did a wide sweeping motion of the greenhouse. "There's a lot here to digest."

"I'm not sure. I need to see how my day goes." He dropped his eyes to study the cement floor. "Can I let you know?"

I was confused. He was acting odd. First almost irritated that I was meeting Dax for coffee, and then his eyes had the sad puppy look that I rarely saw from him. "Sure."

"Um. I have to lock up so you need to leave."

I looked around at the roses. "You'll talk to Alvin about who can take care of these, like watering them?"

He pointed at the wall where a small gauge was attached to a black hose and a water spigot. "It looks like that's covered."

My eyes followed to where he pointed to the path from the ground, upward, and I realized it was an irrigation system. At least the plants wouldn't die from lack of water, and the temperature was regulated too. It would be a shame to have these beautiful plants wither from neglect. "Does anyone in Dean's family want to take over the business? I know he has a couple of sisters down near Portland."

Gage shrugged. "When I contacted Maggie Hartley, one of his sisters, she said someone would be up as soon as they could stay at the house."

I leveled my gaze on him. "When do you think that will be?"

"A week maybe? There is a lot we still don't know."

He held open the door for me to exit the building. I hesitated and took one last look around. On the surface, if I hadn't witnessed the arguments at the festival, I would never have pictured growing roses as a life-threatening occupation, and who knows, maybe it wasn't. But the pieces fit together that it was linked back to this building.

"Gage. Please give serious thought to coming for dinner. As you just said, there is a lot of unknowns. Let me help you. We both know that I have a way of seeing things you don't."

His smile tugged at the corners of his mouth. "And you usually end up in mischief because of just that."

"Stop worrying that I'm going to be in close contact with the murderer. I've learned my lesson. No more following up on hunches alone."

His eyebrow quirked. "And the sun isn't going to shine tomorrow."

The tone of his voice had lightened considerably in the last few minutes, and I was relieved.

"I need to get going," he said. He withdrew a lock from his jacket and placed it on the door.

"I'm going to take one last look around out back, and then I'll take off."

Gage touched my arm. "See, you're already putting yourself in potential danger. We don't know how the killer crept up on Dean, and this was his place. Someone might be lurking in the woods. Get in your car and head back to town."

I hated to admit it, but he was right. My next phone call would be to Nikki to see if she'd come out with me after I got done meeting Dax. I gave Gage a bright smile. "You're right. I need to get back to town. See you tonight at six-ish?"

"Maybe." He walked me to my car and opened the driver's door. "Don't come back here alone. Understood? It's too isolated."

With a lighthearted laugh, I said, "I promise I won't

come back here today without backup." Sliding behind the wheel, I gave him a bright smile. "See you later."

He closed the door and shook his head before saying, "Enjoy your coffee." He turned his back to me and strode to his car.

As I pulled onto the road, I realized he never said the word date. What was that all about? Another puzzle for another day.

Chapter 9
Gage

I watched Lily's car disappear from sight, and a lead weight settled in my gut. She was going on a date with Dax Peters. Sure, it was only coffee, but it could lead to more. I should be the one having a date with her. Pushing the image of them sitting across from each other all cozy-like out of my mind, I refocused on the matter in front of me—solving Dean Hartley's case.

All the physical evidence pointed to a homicide, and he had been faceup with the ladder lying next to him making it almost impossible for him to have fallen onto the pruners. With the confirmation from the medical examiner the trajectory, of the loppers was from below, totally blowing the theory of an accident out of the water.

My cell pinged with an incoming text. Mac was wondering what was keeping me. I started my car and turned in the opposite direction Lily had taken to make the quick drive to Dean's house.

Walking up the short path to the front door, I paused to survey the surrounding area. Mac and Peabody had been over this place with a fine-tooth comb I was sure, but had they walked the well-worn path between the house and the clearing to the greenhouse? I could picture Dean taking it on a regular basis. It was one more area to explore when I was done.

Once inside, I noticed the house was tidy but lacked the touch of anyone who had a sense of design. The perfectly matched brown leather furniture looked as if it was right off a showroom floor. There were no signs of an indentation where a person might have sat on the cushions. There were no family pictures or items littering the tabletops except for the stack of books and a single picture of Dean with his dog next to a recliner chair. Placed on top was a pair of reading glasses and a coaster. I took a closer look and saw a ring of what I guessed might be from a coffee cup. All the signs of a solitary and maybe even lonely life. I shook off the feeling that it reminded me a bit of my place.

I followed the muffled sounds of Mac and Peabody talking in a back room. Upon entering what appeared to be the office, Peabody was sitting in front of a desktop computer, studying a monitor.

"Look right here," she said, pointing to something I couldn't see yet.

"What did you find?" I peered over her shoulder, acknowledging Mac with a brisk nod.

She looked up. "Whoever was at the greenhouse with Hartley had to have known there were cameras in the parking area. We can see Dean in a couple of frames talking to someone but there is nothing from the actual parking lot." She switched views and scanned through the footage several times the normal speed. "This is one hour before and after the estimated time of death."

As usual, Peabody was right. No one other than Dean had been caught on video until Lily and Nikki arrived a short while later; the time stamp was right before she had called me. It looked as if he had a productive afternoon from the time he got home from the festival. What reason he decided to cut shrubs at the end of a day was a question that would never be answered.

"How many different cameras are active?" I asked.

Mac said, "Two in the greenhouse, covering it from end to end. There is another one that covers the two doors in and out of the greenhouse. It captures a couple of feet into the back area, but there is nothing on the house or larger outdoor spaces, and nothing on the parking area or path leading from here to the greenhouse."

"His priority was the roses." It was an observation, and I was sure Mac and Peabody had come to the same conclusion. "What have we learned about the people he argued with at the festival? Was there anything that pinged your radar?"

Peabody said, "Except for Tucker's argument, they all share equal weight of suspicion."

"What do you mean about Tucker?" I looked at one of the walls covered in bulletin boards. Everywhere I looked there was information about cultivating roses, propagating them, or selling them. Dean's sole focus was his business. And it was as if the room told the entire story of his life. Here, there were file cabinets, stacks of papers, and books on roses. This office was the heart of Dean Hartley's home.

She continued. "From what Lily said, they had argued, and Dean gave Tucker money. An educated guess would be somehow Dean took the pruners and hadn't paid for them and when he did, things eased between the two of them. It was just a minor issue."

I nodded, knowing I needed to stop at the hardware store myself to see what the situation had been about. But that still left the entire garden club as a group along with Mike Shaw, Alvin and Ava Springs, and Edie Jenkins.

"What are you thinking, Detective?" Mac asked.

"Hmm." I tapped the whiteboard. "We need to nail down all the garden club members and find out more about this supposed theft of a rose. Why is it important to everyone from a financial point of view? I think once we figure that out, we can narrow the focus on who the most likely suspect is."

"Was Lily at the greenhouse with you earlier?" Peabody said.

"She was, but at this point, she doesn't have a clear picture either. I'm going to swing by her place tonight and talk a few things over."

Mac nudged Peabody, and they both chuckled.

She smirked. "Is dinner involved?"

"She's my best friend, and we frequently have dinner together." I sounded like I had something to hide by the snarky tone of my voice, like I was the one ready to be interrogated. "Why does everyone jump to the same conclusion about me and Lily?"

Peabody put up her hands in surrender. "Just a simple question." Again, Mac bobbed his head in agreement with his partner.

"Pack up the computer and take it down to the station. Keep reviewing old footage to see what you can discover."

Mac said, "It only has a thirty-day storage so with any luck, something will have happened in that time frame."

"Okay. I'm going to the hardware store and check in with Tucker, and then I'll meet you back at the station."

"Sure thing, Detective," Peabody said.

I glanced at my watch and noticed it was almost three. This had taken longer than I thought. "I'm just going to do one final walk-through of the house in case we've over-looked something and then check out the path from here to the greenhouse."

The officers nodded as they were busy shutting the computer down, getting it ready for transport.

The rest of the small ranch house had that sterile, unlived in look except the bedside table in what had been Dean's bedroom. It too had a stack of books and magazines about roses in addition to a crossword puzzle book. I walked around to the other side of the bed to enter the bathroom and on the floor was a nail file, the kind used in a nail salon. A quick guess told me he had at least one friend of the female persuasion. I stepped out the door and called to Mac to come and bag it. It was a small detail, but it could be important. With one final look in the last empty bedroom, I noted nothing seemed out of place, and I was ready to leave. And at least I had stalled long enough so I wouldn't run into Lily and Dax coming out of the coffee shop. Unless they met at the store. The idea of him sitting in the chair that I usually did, having coffee with Lily irked me. Without saying anything to Mac or Peabody, I strode out the front door.

It was almost four when I arrived at the hardware store. Tucker was waiting on a customer who was purchasing paint. I wandered around, looking at the shelves of things I didn't need to purchase when I found myself standing in front of the garden tools. Several different lengths of garden shears were hanging on a wall display. I noticed the pruners that had been responsible for Dean's death were the longest ones for sale.

Tucker said, "Can I help you with something, Gage?"

I spun around. "Hey, Tucker. I don't need any tools, but do you have a minute for a couple of questions? It's about your argument with Dean Hartley on Saturday."

He crossed his arms over his chest and frowned. "I'm surprised it took you this long to stop by."

Tucker's defenses kicked in, and I didn't appreciate his sarcasm, but I understood. This was stressful, especially since I had questioned him two times in the last couple of months regarding a murder. Why everything kept rolling back to the last two months was perplexing. There were bad vibes in the air; that was the only way I could explain it. "I figured you weren't going anywhere, and my questions weren't urgent."

He nodded. "How can I help?" he said, his voice back to normal now.

"Lily mentioned witnessing an argument between you and Dean earlier in the day at the festival. Would you tell me what it was about?"

"Why don't you ask her?" He stuck his hands in his pockets and narrowed his eyes. "She was in here about an hour ago, asking me the same kinds of questions. Seems like if you're going to have her unofficially helping you that you could communicate better."

Inwardly, I groaned. "Lily was here?"

Now he grinned. "Her and Nikki. She wanted to know how Dean got pruners out of my store without paying for them. I don't know about that woman. She just zeros in on something and gets people to open up. I told her the whole story."

He paused as if that was all I needed to hear. "Which was?" I hoped to draw out the rest of his conversation with Lily.

"In hindsight, it wasn't a big deal. I just got annoyed

with him like always. Early Saturday morning he came in and took the loppers off the wall without paying for them. Like he owned the place. I was waiting on a customer and didn't want to be rude, but as soon as I had the chance, I marched over to his booth to get my money. After I said my piece, Dean apologized, explaining he was just in a rush, and I came back to the store." He lifted one shoulder in a nonchalant shrug and his face fell. "Water under the bridge. But I'm glad we cleared the air before the end of the day. With what happened and all."

"You knew him well, then?" I asked.

He stuck his hands in the front pockets of his jeans. "We were friends. He bought most of what he needed for his business through the store. I could order supplies in bulk, and he liked doing business locally. He was a firm believer in supporting other small businesses like his own."

"I hadn't realized you knew him so well."

Tucker looked out the window and got a faraway look in his eyes as if remembering better days. "He was a difficult man to get to know, but once you did, he was a loyal friend. It's still hard to believe he's gone." He looked back at me. "What's going to happen to his business?"

"I contacted his sister, and as soon as we release the buildings and grounds, she's coming up and will make some decisions."

"Good. He poured his life into growing those flowers. It would be a shame to see it go to waste." A scowl flashed over his face. "Who's taking care of them now?"

"I checked on the irrigation system and it seems to be working, and the temperature is consistent too. Everything in the greenhouse seems to be status quo." It was heartening to see Tucker's concern for his friend and gut instinct told me he had nothing to do with the death of Dean. "Tucker, one more thing. Would Dean have tried to propagate a rose from one that had a patent just for profit?"

"No, he was an ethical man." His face split into a grin. "And for the record, now you do sound just like Lily."

Once again, she was one step ahead of me.

Chapter 10
Lily

After talking to Tucker, I was more convinced that Nikki and I had to go out to the greenhouse one more time. This time I wanted to walk the path from Dean's house to where he died and of course take another look around just in case something small had been overlooked or even better, someone had come back to find that USB drive and left a clue as to their identity.

As we got on the road out of town, Nikki asked, "How was coffee with Dax?"

"Huh?" I glanced her way. "Right. My coffee date." I shrugged. "It was okay. He's nice and all, but all he talked about was work. Seems like not much is happening with his case right now since Dean's murder wasn't related to the real estate fraud that is going on."

"No sparks between you?"

"Nada. I was hoping I'd be interested enough in a second date."

"And..." Nikki drawled out.

I laughed. "He started to ask, but I told him I was

meeting you, so effectively, I cut the date short before he could."

Shaking her head, Nikki said, "Poor Dax. You need to come up with something in case he calls you."

I waved my hand as if I were batting away a fly and flashed her a grin. "I just won't answer my phone for the time being. Besides, I'm starting to think this idea of dating to forget about Gage is stupid. Like why can't I ask him out?"

A smile twitched her lips she said, "That's a question only you can answer."

I grew quiet as I contemplated Nikki's response. Knowing she was right and acting on it were two different stories.

"What are we looking for when we get there?"

It was good how she changed the subject. "I have no idea, but I was thinking maybe we could use the finding spell. Like ask for any hidden objects. The only times I've made it work was when I was looking for my shoes that Milo made disappear, but it could work, right?" I could hear the half-hopeful, half-pleading sound in my voice.

Nikki slowly shook her head. "I've never learned that one."

"What? It's in the book."

Half turning in her seat, she gave me a long look. "Each book of *Practical Beginnings* is personal to the witch. I may have that spell somewhere in my book, but I haven't needed it so it's never appeared."

I glanced at her before slowing down to turn onto the gravel driveway. "Our books aren't the same?"

"No. They're passed down through families, but even what you're learning isn't how Mimi or your dad learned witchcraft."

I backed the car into a spot one parking space away from the greenhouse. For some strange reason, I felt as if the air had left my body. "All witches learn differently, like the book knows what we need and when we need it? Interesting." Looking around the woods, everything was still. Once again, I had the impression they were waiting to reclaim the land. I shivered against what I told myself was a chill. "I'm going to try the spell. It can't hurt, right?" I snapped my fingers. "What about the summoning spell, you know where I can summon the killer to come out here."

Nikki grabbed my forearm and squeezed. "Promise me you will not do that. Ever. For that we'd need police backup, and I am positive you didn't let Gage know we were coming out here, did you?"

"Well, no." The words came out in a super slow drawl. "I promised him that I wouldn't come out here alone, and I kept that one."

"I'm sure he thought that would be a deterrent, that I'm not crazy enough to jump in a car each time you ask to go to a murder scene." She shook her head.

We both knew once my mind was made up, there was little anyone could do to change it. "Look on the bright side. I'll promise to not do the summoning spell."

Nikki pushed her door open and grumbled. "Hardly the bright side and you know, there are days I wish you hadn't gotten your powers. Life was simpler when you were just an average mortal."

I closed my door and looked over the roof of the car. "Are you calling me average?"

Laughing, she said, "You're right; that was insulting." She strode around the front of the car and said, "Let's go track down your clues and get out of here. And when we're done, we'll stop at my house. I made a tart for your dinner tonight." She gave me a wink and a grin. "I'm sure a handsome detective will be swinging by and not to talk about the case, but to discover just how good your date with Dax was."

I groaned and trudged forward, my leather boots heavy like I was walking through wet cement. "Can we stop talking about Dax?"

She gave me a light punch on the arm. "Only after you ask Gage out."

I decided to drop the subject and focus on why we were out here. To find clues. I didn't like that so much anger had gotten out of control and three people in our town had died. The only good thing was I had helped solve two of the murders, and with some luck and skill, I could help Gage wrap this one up too.

I trained my eyes at the ground as we made slow progress walking around the greenhouse. It was like we were walking in a slow grid pattern again; Nikki was next to me doing the same thing. So far, we hadn't discovered anything.

It was hard to believe it had just been a few days since the festival and Dean was alive and arguing with members of the garden club and Mike Shaw. He was next on my list of people to bump into, and then I needed to reach out to the rest of the club members. I stopped where I had first noticed Dean's body. The image was crystal clear in my mind. He was lying face up in a pool of red, pruners jutting from his body. I closed my eyes and pictured the scene again. Something about it was bothering me, but I couldn't put my finger on it, at least not yet.

Snapping my fingers, I said, "Nikki, do you remember seeing a hat on the ground near the body?"

She shook her head. "No, I was too freaked out. He was my first dead person up close."

I touched her arm, offering a small comfort. "It was a shock, but you don't remember the hat?"

"No."

I pulled out my phone and scrolled through the pictures I had taken.

Nikki leaned over my shoulder and gasped. "You took pictures?"

With a sharp look at her, I said, "Of course. Gage would never give me access to crime scene photos after the fact, so I just snapped a couple." I tapped my screen. "Look, there is a fedora style straw hat near the ladder."

Tapping out a quick text, I asked Gage, "Have you identified who the straw hat belongs to that was next to the ladder?"

It zipped off with a whoosh. If he had his phone handy, it wouldn't take long for him to get back to me, and the ping of an incoming text was confirmation.

What hat?

That was an indirect answer to my question. I jotted off a text before slipping the phone back in my pocket. *I'll tell you later.*

Nikki popped her hands on her hips and did a slow three-sixty turn. "If he didn't see it, maybe the wind picked it up. Let's search the area."

"There's a better way." I closed my eyes and slowed my breathing as I had done the first time I learned the summoning spell. Picturing the fedora in my mind's eye, silently I rode up the escalator that appeared in front of me. The kitten version of Milo was resting on an all-white couch. I reached out and scratched between the kitten's ears and a look of kitty contentment appeared on its face. I whispered, "Please guide me to where the straw hat is located in the bushes that was near Dean Hartley. As you will, so it shall be." The kitten dipped its chin, and I rode the escalator back down. Opening my eyes, I waited to see if I would be pulled in any specific direction, but nothing had changed.

"Where to?" Nikki asked.

Despite being able to do some magic, this particular spell was finicky. It worked in its own time, and there was nothing I could do to speed up the process. "Let's keep looking for clues and forget about the hat for now."

She understood that magic sometimes took a while to kick in and without further questions continued to walk beside me. We circled the yellow tape that still outlined the grassy area, the bright-red spot that had been there was now a dull rusty red. My heart twisted thinking of the poor man bleeding without anyone to help him. Too bad his leaf reading had come true. How was it possible that I had been right? I longed to talk with Aunt Mimi. I'd ask her to come down to the bookstore tomorrow and help me sort out what seemed like my ability to read tea leaves. Was there a way I could have protected Dean? I didn't know, but I needed to be sure.

"There's nothing out here, Lily. We should head back to town. It's getting cold, and you said you still wanted to see Alvin and Ava Springs, since they had been a part of the group from the garden club arguing with him."

I looked up and saw the concern in her eyes.

She said, "You're getting really invested in solving this when it might be dangerous. You've come close to becoming a ghost twice, and it's not something I want to think about."

"I need to help. It's not something I can explain but"—I

tapped the center of my chest—"it's in here, urging me to keep looking."

"Sweetie," Nikki said.

She only called me that when she wanted to change my mind after I had made it up. "I know what you're saying, but if Steve needed your help, would you quit trying?"

"There is a difference between what Steve and Gage do for a living. One is a mechanic, and the other is a cop. One can fix an engine, and the other has the skills to solve a crime."

In my gut, she made sense but there was something about the case that I was drawn to. It had to have been the reading; it's the only thing that was different this time. I rubbed my hands over my shirtsleeves. The sun was beginning to set, and shadows were creeping closer. "I'm ready to go back to town if you are."

Nikki looped her arm through the crook of mine and half steered, half pulled me in the direction of my car. Hopefully this time there wouldn't be an animal standing between us and it.

As we rounded the last corner, a large black four-door sedan pulled in and parked in front of the greenhouse. We froze in our steps, unsure if we should keep walking or wait to see who got out.

I sighed with relief as Alvin and Ava opened the car doors. They were bickering about who had a key to get in when I called out, "Hello." At least I wasn't going to have to go in search of them.

Their heads snapped so hard it was surprising they didn't pop off like erasers on pencils.

"What are you doing here?" Ava demanded, her lips curled into a snarl.

"Oh, you know, just looking around." I squeezed Nikki's

arm close to my body in solidarity more than anything. "I could ask the same about you too."

Ava sniffed and her chin tilted up like she was the owner of the place and not a trespasser. "Dean and I were very close. My brother and I came out to check on the flowers." She narrowed her eyes and glared at me. "It would seem we have more of a right to be here than you."

"How do you plan on getting inside? The greenhouse is locked, and Detective Erikson made sure the building was secured with an extra padlock, protecting all the evidence."

Ava paled and reached out for Alvin's arm to steady her as she stumbled. "Does that mean they suspect," she dropped her voice to a hoarse whisper and said, "foul play?"

It was my turn to throw out the haughty act. "Well, it is common occurrence, given the circumstances of Dean's death, that it would be investigated as a possible homicide." I couldn't help but wonder how on earth she could pretend to be blindsided. Especially since I'd bet the last book in my store that the brother and sister duo weren't dropping by to merely check on the plants. I wanted to fire off a sharp retort, but I held my tongue. No sense in giving away details of the incident, and if either of them or as a duo had a hand in Dean's death, no sense in tipping mine.

"Once Gage is done with the investigation, it will be a matter of public record how Dean died and the additional circumstances around it."

Ava regained her composure and Alvin's remained stoic. "I think we'll just walk around for a bit—you know, stretch our legs."

"We'll join you," I said as we turned in the direction of the grassy area again. This was my opportunity to see if I could unearth what had happened at the festival between the garden club group and Dean.

Nikki opened her mouth, but I gave her a wink, hoping she would follow my lead. With a slight nod of her head, she acquiesced. We walked next to Alvin and Ava. I didn't speak yet, letting the tension between us relax as we strolled. Pouncing right away was something Milo would encourage me to do, but not with these two; they'd clam up in a heartbeat.

"It really is tragic what happened out here," Nikki's voice was filled with compassion. "Had you all been friends long?"

Alvin said, "At least ten years. Once Dean dove into roses as a business, we didn't see as much of him, but he was still an active member of our club. Some of the other members are as passionate about roses as Dean was."

Ava was nodding. "The delicate blooms and the varieties are astounding. Most people think of roses by colors—white, red, yellow. You know the standards to mark certain occasions, but there is so much more to them. It's a serious and complex business."

I nodded, pulling the Gage trick of giving someone time to talk, and hoped it would yield a bit more information.

She continued. "Some people, like Mike Shaw, accused Dean of propagating roses with an attempt to infringe on a patent. But I know for a fact he was working on a rose that would have a faster recycle blooming variety. Since he's a greenhouse grower, he needs plants that continue to reproduce in our northern climate."

"A faster recycle?" I asked, unsure what exactly she meant.

"Yes," Ava said. "About fifty years ago, there was a patent granted on a red rose that would bloom for Christmas sales and then quickly bloom again for Valentine's Day. But Dean wanted an even quicker cycle and not just in reds. Now, I know there are varieties in all colors, but what he did with growing flowers was something special. They had the best smell and seemed to last forever as cut flowers."

Alvin chimed in. "It might have worked if someone hadn't started to spread the rumor he was doing something unethical. It got folks all in an uproar, and then it bubbled over at the festival where he had the new plant on display. Not as cut flowers mind you, just the plant, and it wasn't for sale."

The four of us were now standing in the clearing with nothing to look at other than the yellow crime scene tape fluttering slightly as the wind kicked up. It was all quiet just as it had been when Nikki and I walked through moments before. "Who started the rumor?" I asked.

"Mike Shaw. He loves to stir up trouble, and he's had an axe to grind with Dean for years." Alvin's voice was harsh as he stole a glance at Ava.

Why did he keep looking at his sister, and what specifically did she have to do with all of this? I had many more questions that needed answers. With Alvin and Ava connected at the hip, there was no way to get any information out of her.

Ava said, "Now wait, it wasn't Dean's fault. He was the innocent party in all of this. All he was doing was making a living by growing the best roses he could."

By the look of displeasure that flashed over Alvin's face, Ava coming to his defense so quickly was a new wrinkle in all of this. Why did Alvin not like Dean?

"Why do you always defend that guy? He didn't give a whit about your feelings. Not that you seemed to mind, mooning over him the way you did." The scowl of displeasure turned into disgust.

Ava stamped her foot on the grass, and the effect was lessened as it didn't make a sound. Her point was made though as she jabbed a perfectly manicured finger in bright pink in her brother's face. "Dean Hartley was my friend, and once upon a time, he was your friend too."

It was obvious Ava didn't care what she said with me and Nikki around, but Alvin hissed, "Be quiet. You shouldn't be talking about our personal business in front of these two."

Ava snorted. "I don't care who knows how I felt about Dean. I loved him, and we are both adults and single. Dating him made me happy for the first time in years."

She turned her back on him and stalked to where their car was parked. Without another word to us, Alvin hurried after her.

I crossed my arms over my chest and watched them get into the car, still bickering, and pull from the parking area, kicking up gravel in their haste.

Nikki said, "Now what do you make of that?"

I glanced her way. "Alvin just became my primary suspect."

Chapter 11
Lily

Once I got back to town and dropped Nikki off at her place and picked up the tart, I headed home via the fish market. I had been neglecting Milo the last few days and knew a nice piece of fish would go a long way to getting back into his good graces. I walked through the back door, calling for him, and he trotted into the kitchen as if he was actually happy to see me.

"Milo, I bought fish for our dinner tonight." I held the brown paper bag aloft.

"Great, you bought fish. It's not like you caught it yourself." That deep kitty growl was less than an enthusiastic welcome home. "Is Detective Cutie coming for dinner too?"

I hung my jacket by the kitchen door and said, "Yes, I think so. We need to talk about the case, but before he gets here, I'd like to run a few things by you."

He hopped up onto the chair and tipped his head. "About time. I've been doing my own legwork."

"Why didn't you tell me?" I washed and dried my hands and withdrew ingredients from the refrigerator to make a coleslaw.

"You didn't ask."

Ouch. I had no idea that my familiar could be spot-on. "I'm sorry, Milo. Things have been wonky, and I haven't been able to get a handle on why someone would have wanted Dean dead until this afternoon."

"Maybe if you had been reading your book, *Practical Beginnings*, things would have become clear. We've discovered one thing about your powers since Saturday." He stopped talking and concentrated on washing his face with his paw.

I waited half a minute, which dragged on forever until I couldn't stand being left hanging. "Milo!"

He paused and gave me his typical baleful look. "You mean you haven't figured it out yourself?" He shook his head. "This is why you need to read the book and practice every day, not just when you feel like it."

I needed to ask Aunt Mimi and Nikki if their familiars were borderline rude at times. "No. If I had, do you think I'd need you to prompt me?"

"You have an innate ability to read tea leaves. You knew what was in store for Dean. Sadly, it was too late. That is a highly sought-after talent in our world. Very few people can do it well and on their first attempt." He held up his paw as if he were going to give me a high five. "Bravo." He dropped his paw back to the chair seat. "If you had..."

I interrupted him, "Read the book." I hoped my voice didn't sound as weary as I felt when Milo talked about my training manual.

"Exactly. Tonight, after your dinner guest leaves, we're going to open it and see what you need to learn next."

"That means I have to go back to the store and pick it up. Why don't we just do that tomorrow."

Milo lightly jumped down to the kitchen floor. "The

book is in your office. There's no need to go back to the store tonight."

I bent over and scooped Milo into my arms. "I'm certain I left the book at the store."

He butted his head against my chin, and I scratched behind his ears. "Which is why you never work on your magic. You've been busy, and I took it upon myself to get it here, where you can practice uninterrupted." He squirmed in my arms, and I set him on the floor.

"Wait. How did you manage that?"

"My dear witch, I can't tell you all my secrets; you'd be bored with me in an instant. This way, I get to keep you guessing for years to come."

He stalked from the room, and I called after him, "You're going to get tired trying to stay one step ahead of me."

The back door closed, and I whirled around. Gage was standing in the kitchen, holding a large brown paper bag and grinning. "Milo giving you attitude again?"

I shook my head while my heart rate ticked up from his smile. "You have no idea." How much of my conversation had he heard? I was sure the door was tightly closed. "When did you get here?"

"Two seconds ago. Long enough to see Milo trot from the room, and I'm not sure what you said to him, but it's cute how you talk to him like he understands exactly what you're saying."

Relief washed over me; tension hadn't lingered between us from my date with Dax, and the Milo conversation was a non-issue. Since he only heard a few words, it hadn't sounded like it was a long, one-way conversation with my familiar. "He's good company." My eyes trailed to the bag. "What did you bring?"

He set it on the counter. "I swung by the Clam Bake and picked up a those twice-baked potatoes you like and of course a few rolls too."

My mouth began to water with the knowledge the rolls would be golden brown, smothered in garlic butter, and the loaded potatoes were filled with a blend of cheese, sour cream, and bacon bits. Not diet friendly but at least the baked fish would balance out the rest of the meal. I tipped my head and grinned. "No coleslaw?"

"Is that something I'd ever forget?" He quipped. "If the rest of the world knew how good it was, Fred Wickshire would be in the slaw biz, instead of fish."

"I'm glad you picked some up. I was going to make a bowl, but his is much better than mine." I opened the bag and began to unpack it. I needed to stay busy while my brain whirled as I pondered what Milo said regarding the tea leaves. Is that something I could broach with Gage? He didn't seem to think it was totally ridiculous on Saturday.

As was our routine, he took plates from the cabinet and silverware from the drawer. "Penny for your thoughts?"

"What?" I looked up, realizing I had gotten very quiet while I prepped the fish. "Sorry. I was thinking about Saturday when I read Dean's tea leaves. I should have made him listen that danger lurked; he might still be alive now."

Setting the plates and utensils on the table, he leaned against the counter. He was so close to me I could hear his heart beating. "You really believe the reading was genuine?"

I took a step back. My heartbeat kicked up. Being this close to Gage was distracting, and I needed a clear head to answer him. Maybe now was the ideal moment I should confide in him I was a witch, but the thought evaporated quickly. Another day when we weren't in the throes of me trying to help him track down a murderer. "Yes. I do think there is information in the universe that guides us. It isn't linear, which can't be explained by science. Many instances have indicated that people are sensitive to information or knowledge that others are not."

"Like ghosts?"

I shook my head. "I don't know about ghosts for sure, but I think spirits can get stuck in limbo. Don't you ever smell your grandma's pie baking or your uncle's pipe smoke? That could be a ghost, but I'm talking about when someone wants to have their tea leaves read, there is an intention to look at life differently, through a different lens if you will."

He nodded, his mouth dropping into that thoughtful twist, his eyes half-closed. "I can see where that might come into play, like when I have a hunch that plays out during an investigation?"

"Exactly. Some of that is drawing on your experience as a detective, but the universe is also talking to you, and you need to listen."

Nodding, a smile began to grow on his lips. "Okay. I can agree to that. But what does that have to do with the case? Unless you read another person's leaves that indicated they were about to do something horrible. Did you?"

I washed and dried my hands as I thought of all the people who had asked for a reading. "No, and none of the garden club members came by for a reading. A few bought tea, but most people regarded my part of the event as a lark. Which is perfectly fine. But Dean was hoping for a good report, so his intentions were focused on a positive outcome." I dropped my chin, wishing I had been wrong.

"You couldn't have stopped what happened. Someone wished Dean harm, and it would have happened no matter what the leaves said."

His words did nothing to console me. The only way to

put things to right was to solve the case. "Nikki and I went back to the greenhouse late this afternoon."

"I knew you would." There wasn't a smile on his face or in his voice, just resignation. "Did you discover anything we missed earlier?" He picked up the plates and set the table before opening the pantry door to pull out the chalkboard stand that I had tucked out of sight. He really did know me.

I wiped the board clean and handed him the chalk. "Would you write while I finish dinner?"

"What should I start with?" he asked.

"Alvin and Ava Springs should be at the top of the list. They showed up at the greenhouse today and they were looking for something. I wonder if it was the USB drive?"

Gage drew a line down the center and on the left side he wrote down their names. On the right, he added USB in all caps. He continued to add Tucker Gleason, Mike Shaw, Edie Jenkins, and added the pruners on the right.

"Add sun hat to the right too."

He gave me a curious look but did as I asked. "Anything else?"

I slid a grill pan of fish with tomatoes, olives, and seasoning into the oven and washed my hands all the while studying the board. "We could list all the garden club members, but so far no one has piqued my interest like Ava and Alvin."

"Tell me what they said today." He placed the chalk on the kitchen table and sat down, and I joined him.

"Nikki and I were just leaving, and we were joking about how we didn't need another surprise like Brutus sitting by the car. When we came around the corner, Alvin and Ava drove up, and they were arguing."

He cocked a brow and leaned closer to me. "Were you able to discover what they were fighting about?"

"It was about a key. When I asked them what they were doing there, they said they wanted to check on the plants in the greenhouse. I informed them it was padlocked by you and no one had a key. And then I did the Gage method, giving them time to ramble in conversation. I encouraged a walk around the back, and they jumped on it. Turns out Mike Shaw was very upset that Dean was trying to develop a rose that bloomed more frequently. It sounds like it would have been a game changer in the industry. But the real kicker came when Ava confessed she had strong feelings for Dean and it was apparent Alvin was not happy about that. And she even mentioned Alvin and Dean had a falling out. Unfortunately, she left in a huff before she told us the rest, but after that entire exchange, Alvin moved to the top of my list."

"Huh. I wish I had been there for that conversation. I would have had a lot of questions." He tapped his chin with his index finger. "You said they wanted to go inside the greenhouse?"

"They did. The excuse was they wanted to make sure Dean's plants were okay. But if they were close, wouldn't they have known he had a system to keep everything watered and running smoothly?"

"They should." Gage leaned back in his chair and studied the chalkboard. "I agree that Alvin hopped up the list, but what about the fingernail that was found at the scene?"

"Wait." I could picture Ava pointing her finger at Alvin. "Ava's nails are painted that same shade of pink."

"As the nail we found? Interesting."

The excitement in Gage's voice was a relief. The information I had gathered today was helping him put the pieces together. "Yes and no. Changing nail color takes an hour at the salon." I had to wonder who else in the garden club had their nails done since I was convinced this was all centered around the group.

The timer on the oven buzzed, and I said, "Dinner's ready." It was an anticlimax to the conversation. I crossed the room and pulled the pan from the oven. Gage put a star next to Alvin's name and took a quick picture of the board as I smiled to myself.

"I appreciate the information and thank you for taking Nikki with you today. There is something about this case that is bothering me, and people in town will know you're looking into things. Make sure you stay vigilant and don't go off following a hunch on your own."

His voice had a pleading tone that caused my heart to skip a beat. The space between us evaporated as I wrapped my arms around his waist and squeezed. I might not be able to tell him how I felt, but his concern for me was comforting and elating at the same time. I kissed his cheek. "I'll be careful, I promise."

He held me tight. "Good." The word came out as a croak which made me love him even more.

"Let's eat before Milo comes out and helps himself to our dinner." I relaxed my arms and stepped back. A flash of something slipped from Gage's eyes before I could figure out what it was. Too bad there wasn't a spell to decipher what he was thinking. Maybe Milo was right and working on new spells would be just what I needed as a distraction. As I thought of my familiar, he stalked into the kitchen and tipped his head in that all-knowing look, and I swear he winked at me.

Chapter 12
Gage

Driving home after a wonderful dinner with Lily was disheartening. I wanted to ask her about the date with Dax, even though I didn't have any right to ask. I needed to know if she wanted to go out with him again or if instead, she'd go out with me. It was stupid and I certainly had no reason to impose myself on her that way. We were best friends and someday maybe I'd finally accept that was the way our lives were supposed to be. And then the idea of her putting herself out there to solve this crime was another burden to carry. Lately, it seemed, danger was right around every corner. There wasn't anything I wouldn't do to protect her, but standing on the sidelines of her life hobbled my efforts. I should talk to Dax and see how things went from his point of view. My shoulders straightened. Maybe he didn't want to go out with Lily again. But what if she wanted to date him and Dax rejected her? I wanted her to be happy even if it wasn't with me.

The next morning, I eased into my parking space at the police station and took the front steps two at a time, pulling the door open. I entered my office and hung up my jacket without meeting another human. Doing routine things helped clear my head, and I needed to look at Alvin with fresh eyes. I must have overlooked something. With Lily's assessment of him and the telltale indicator he was trying to get into the greenhouse yesterday, something was wonky. I could feel it in my gut—the murder was linked to that one rosebush that Dean had on display. I smacked my hand on my forehead. Was that plant even still in the greenhouse? And who could go out there with me and tell the truth?

Running down the list of suspects from Lily's board, since my notes were in desperate need of updating, my thoughts turned to Tucker Gleason. He was so far from the top of the suspect list and he had been a good friend for years. Maybe he'd have time to take a trip out to the greenhouse with me. Surely, he knew the plant all the buzz was about. I picked up the desk phone and called the hardware store. After a couple of rings, he answered.

"Tucker, it's Gage Erikson." I hoped the use of just my name would make this call less official.

"Good morning, Detective. How can I help you?"

The distinct cool tone in his voice was unmistakable. It was to be expected since Tucker knew he was on the suspect list, even if it was at the bottom. No sense beating around the bush. "I was hoping you would have some free time to take a ride out to Hartley's greenhouse with me this morning."

Without hesitation, he asked, "Does this mean I'm no longer a suspect?"

I dropped to my chair and leaned back. "I have found no evidence to suggest you had anything to do with Dean's death, other than own a hardware store which sells hedge cutters. Which isn't a crime. But in full transparency, you're the only person I trust answering a few questions for me." I didn't come right out and say he was not a suspect, but with any luck, he'd take what I said as confirmation and respect that I do trust him to help me.

He cleared his throat, "What time are you thinking of going?"

I did a fist pump straight up in the air but remained even-keeled. "When it's convenient for you."

"Let me see if I can get someone to watch the store. I don't like to close during regular hours."

"Understood." I wanted to give him someone to call, but everyone I could think of was either working or a suspect in my investigation. "I hate to ask, but when you do find someone, can you keep why you need to step away confidential?"

"Can do, Detective."

I heard the decided upbeat tone in his voice now, and I wondered if he stood a little taller knowing that I was extending my trust.

"I don't think Nate's gone fishing today. He mentioned something about letting his second-in-command run the boat for the day. Between you and me, since it came out that he and Mimi got hitched, he's been wanting to spend more time on land and less on that lobster boat."

I chuckled. "He waited a long time to marry her, and I can't say that I blame him for wanting to stick closer to shore to be with her."

"Give me an hour and swing by the store. Unless you want me to meet you out there?"

"Thanks, Tucker. I'll pick you up in front of the store in my truck so it doesn't look like police business. I appreciate your help."

"Glad to do it." The older man hung up without saying goodbye which was fine. Tucker had always been a man of few words unless he deemed them important.

I propped my cowboy boots on the desk and tented my fingers together, thinking about what we had said about Nate and Mimi. It reminded me a little of my situation with Lily. Best of friends with me waiting for the opportunity just like Nate did with Mimi. They had spent years dancing around being together and then ran off and got married in secret. Was that going to be me and Lily in thirty years? I dropped my feet to the floor, and my boots hit the ground with a decided thud. After I got back to town, I was going to the Cozy Nook Bookshop and ask Lily to go on a real date with me. Satisfied with my decision, I crossed my office to the whiteboard and withdrew my phone so I could write down the details that Lily and I compiled last night.

Tucker was able to contact Nate, who had been happy to cover the store.

As we drove out of town, he glanced my way. "What do you need from me regarding the flowers? I'm better at selling fertilizer and other supplies than I am growing anything. I have a brown thumb."

"I'm hoping you can take a look around, see if the potted rose that caused such a fuss at the festival is in the greenhouse. Also, you know everything Dean bought from you, so I'm hoping you might be able to see if something seems out of place."

"You know he kept everything organized down to the smallest item. I'll be able to tell you if anything is out of the ordinary." He nodded. "Yup, he was good that way, buying local for most all he could. He was always saying small businesses should support other small businesses. Helps us all when we stick together."

"I'm getting a conflicting picture of him. On the one

hand, he seemed like a curmudgeon, but then you tell me he was a good customer and friend."

"Dean was a complicated man. I think it came from spending so much time with the flowers and not a lot of social interaction. Even with his family, he was distant. Did you know he had his heart broken a while back? But that's just a hunch on something odd he said once."

I slowed and pulled into the parking area of the greenhouse. "What was that?" I asked as I turned my car off.

"He said women are like roses. They're beautiful but can also draw blood if you're not careful." Tucker gave me a long look. "To me that says the man got pricked real bad."

I thought of Lily. Did she have thorns or was she a smooth-stemmed variety? I knew she was a complicated woman, but that was part of her appeal. Each layer of her was like another flower petal.

"Come on," I said and locked the truck after Tucker got out. We walked around the outside of the building to the back. I wanted his reaction to the crime scene, bright-yellow tape and all.

Tucker's steps slowed as we rounded the corner, and he stopped. He turned, looking right and left. "He was found over there?"

I walked closer to where the body had been. "Here." I pointed to where the ladder was found. "The ladder was lying next to him."

"And he was on his back?" His words came out slow and halting. Being this close to a murder had a way of making most people experience moments of shock. Tucker wasn't any different, and the raw emotions emanating off him confirmed he wasn't the person I was going to charge with the crime.

"Yes."

"If he had fallen from the ladder, he probably would have landed on his back." He pointed to where the ladder had been. "Do you know if the extension sections had been secured with bungee cords? He claimed it made it easier for him to carry them—no sliding sections. If he had been on the ladder, he would have tied it off and never have fallen and gotten stabbed."

That was something I hadn't considered. "Thank you. Very good observation. I'll check on the cords when I get back to the station." This cemented even further why I needed him to look around. "Let's go inside." I withdrew my keys and found the bright-silver one for the new padlock I had in place. It was the best way to protect the contents of the building.

I went in first and flipped the light switch and rows of incandescent bulbs illuminated the large space. Even with the grow lights on, there were some dark corners of the building. The scent in the warm humid air was sweet, like a bottle of expensive perfume. "Take your time looking around, and if you see anything out of place or you don't find the potted rose from the festival, let me know. And don't touch anything, Tucker, just in case. I'd rather not find your fingerprints in the mix."

"Got it." He walked to the farthest point in the space, the workbench and shelves full of bottles and bags. Without real gardening experience, it was more like trying to read a book in a foreign language to me.

"Gage, come look at this." He waved me down the nearest row. "I think I've found something." He gestured to a journal jutting out from under a brown bag with the hardware store logo. "Since this is still here, I thought it might have been overlooked."

A frown settled on my face. How had Peabody or Mac

missed this? I pulled a latex glove from my jacket pocket and put it on, being careful to slide the bag out of the way while keeping it upright. I'd look at that next. Flipping through the pages, I was surprised to see it was more of a personal journal than business records. It had dates and cryptic notes, mostly with abbreviations and initials. On the last few pages dated the week leading up to the harvest festival, I slowed to read them more carefully.

Wednesday, GC dropped by with MS, leading the blood-thirsty pack, each person demanding a cutting of my hybrid. Fat chance.

Thursday, A and E came, said they saw my side and seemed to understand. A wanted to get together, but I'm in no mood to juggle her hopes for a future.

Friday, A and E came over. Did they really think I'd give up or in that easily? Tomorrow will be exciting...

Saturday, big day. More later.

That was the last entry, presumably due to his death. But which *A* came back to see him and why?

Tucker was reading over my shoulder. "GC is probably the garden club, MS would be Mike Shaw since he's pretty active with the group, and of course *A*, *A*, and *E* are Alvin, Ava, and Edie. Those three are as thick as thieves. Usually when you see one, you see all of them."

Gage thought about that, and it was interesting since yesterday Lily hadn't mentioned Edie being with the brother and sister duo. "What did the garden club expect to be cut in on? The profits or how Dean was able to produce the new rose?"

He shrugged. "It could be almost anything. But since they wanted cuttings, I would guess one of them wanted to beat him to the patent office. They're a pretty tight group and if they thought any of them could benefit financially from gardening, some would be happy for Dean, but others would want a slice of the action. Especially Mike Shaw. I wouldn't trust him from here to that door." He bobbed his head in the direction of the side door closest to us. "He's the kind of man who wants the easy road to riches."

With a snort, I said, "Then why was he dabbling in flowers? Surely, there is a better get-rich plan?"

"There's money to be made. He may want the easiest route, but he doesn't want to work hard to get it." Tucker scanned the shelves next to the bench. "All this looks pretty normal except Dean should have been more careful putting different chemicals in smaller unmarked bottles. But I'm sure he knew what was where. Like I said, he was exact in everything he did."

To my untrained eye, the shelves looked to be in disarray. "There is a method to this storage system?"

Tucker pointed to the first section and explained what all the items were for, then he did the same with each remaining section, explaining what was toxic to plants in full concentration and what should be diluted for safety. "Like I said, well laid out and in a logical order."

I was going to take his word for it. "Do you notice anything at all that seems out of the ordinary?"

He pointed to the hardware store bag. "This might seem an odd thing for me to say, but Dean believed in using reusable bags or none. So, this bag wasn't his."

"Come on. Everyone uses a paper sack."

He shook his head. "Not Dean."

With my glove-covered hand, I pulled the bag closer. Inside was a red bottle top and a receipt for a couple of bucks. I showed it to Tucker. "Any idea what this was for?"

Taking a closer look, he said, "This isn't from my store.

All my receipts print with Tucker's Hardware across the top."

I pulled out the bottle top. "And this?"

"Soda bottle maybe?" He shrugged. "Gage, it's just trash, nothing more. Whoever brought it, left it behind knowing Dean would have recycled both as soon as he had the chance."

I put the bottle top and receipt back in the bag. Then I pulled out my phone and took a few pictures of the journal in place, before I slipped it into an evidence bag I kept in my other jacket pocket. Sometimes Lily referred to my jacket as the Mary Poppins version of police jackets. With one final look around, I had to wonder what it was that Alvin and Ava wanted to see in here.

"Gage. One last thing. The rose plant you were asking about, it's right over there." I followed to where he was pointing and in the middle of the greenhouse in the center of the tables filled with roses was a bright-blue pot. Tucker was right, that looked like the same pot that was at the festival. "Good to know that it is safe."

Tucker said, "For now."

Chapter 13
Lily

I placed the open book of *Practical Beginnings* on the counter at the bookshop, and Milo promptly sprawled across the pages. "How am I supposed to practice this disappearing spell if I can't see the words?" I slid his body to one side, and he wriggled right back into place.

"You've read it a hundred times since last night after your detective left. If you don't have it memorized by now, you probably won't. So, ignore the book and make one up yourself to accomplish the same goal." He rolled onto his back, displaying his belly. "Any chance of a good scratch?"

"I do not have time to stand here and rub your tummy." I walked over to the door and flipped the sign to OPEN. "And thanks for the vote of confidence that I can just wing a spell." I looked over my shoulder to see if Milo had moved, but he had made the open pages of the book his new bed. "I can't just start making up spells and expect them to work." My shoulders were weary. I had not become a successful and accomplished witch in the last three months. I could barely manage the handful of spells I knew. It took a lot of concentration to find an object. I could levitate a feather easily but nothing else, except when I got the broom to fly up and give me time to escape from being tossed over a widow's walk onto the cliffs below. But the one I could do best—I could summon people to me. I'd been able to call Gage and Aunt Mimi to me on two separate occasions which had been a lifesaver, literally. The one high point so far this morning was Milo not saying, *Read the book.*

"Why the long face, my favorite witch?"

I crossed the room and dropped to one of the reading chairs, ignoring his comment about me being his favorite. "I'm a failure as a witch. I struggle with all my spells except summoning. And this disappearing spell. When will something like that come in handy?" Looking at Milo reminded me even more that my failure was complete. "It took forever to discover I was a witch after adopting you from the shelter and now, well, I just can't pretend any longer. Becoming an accomplished witch like Aunt Mimi or Nikki just isn't in the cards. I started way too late."

Milo hopped down from his spot on the book and padded over to me, jumping into my lap. His deep-green eyes locked on mine. "Now you listen up. Today you're a good witch. You're able to do advanced spells that, for some reason, the book keeps showing you. Levitating a broom and making it fly was downright epic."

I could feel the blush rise in my cheeks when he talked about my time stuck with a crazy person.

"And you saved Gage when that sign collapsed on him. That was not a beginner sleight of hand. He was in grave danger, and you remained calm and did what needed to be done."

Slowly, I said, "I did." Feeling a little better, I kissed the top of his soft gray head. "But why can't I get this spell?"

He did his version of a cat shrugging his shoulders and

tipped his head. "Every time you open that book to learn something, it's out of order. If I didn't know any better, I would think it knows what you need to learn to keep you safe. If that's true, then you must learn how to make something disappear. It could save a life, maybe even yours."

I was just about to ask a question when the door opened and Edie walked in, scanning the space, her face lighting up when she saw me. "Good morning, Lily. Just the person I was hoping to see."

I got up from the chair as Milo hopped to the floor. "Good morning to you, Edie. How can I help you today?" I couldn't remember the last time she had come into the bookstore by herself. Usually Ava was with her, but this could be an opportunity to get a little more information about what had gone on between Alvin and Dean.

She glanced around the spacious book-filled room. "I was hoping to find a book on organic flower gardening." She gave me a bright but seemingly forced smile. "We all need to do our part to save the Earth."

I gestured to a row of books to the left of where we stood. "There should be just what you're looking for down there. Third shelf in the middle."

She looked in the direction I pointed and back to me. "Would you mind showing me? I want to make sure I get everything that I came in for. I'm sure you understand."

That was a cryptic response, but of course the customer was always right, even if I found her a tad odd. "I'm happy to help." I led the way down the row of books and took a couple from the shelf and handed them to her. "These are all excellent and focused on flowers. If you are interested, I have some on vegetables too."

"No need for that. I buy all my vegetables from Marshall Stone's place. He has an amazing selection, so why would I attempt to duplicate his efforts when I can focus on beauty. In fact, I often sell flowers from my garden to Marshall for his stand."

I tipped my head at that interesting tidbit. "Did Dean do the same?"

"All the garden club members had some sort of an arrangement with Marshall. There's no way he could grow vegetables and flowers with only one helper. It's a great solution, don't you think? It's like small businesses helping each other."

And there was the carrot I was looking for. "I didn't realize you had a flower business in addition to Dean's?" Edie still hadn't opened the books in her arms, and it wasn't a stretch to realize the books were an excuse to talk about what was going on with the investigation. But it wasn't like I was privy to all the details. What I knew was mostly common knowledge.

"Not like Dean. I love growing flowers and when I have extra cuttings, I run them out to the farm stand. But Dean, he had a thriving business." She looked around and dropped her voice. "I'm not one to gossip, but did you know that Mike Shaw wanted to edge Dean out of the rose business? He had all these great ideas, but Dean was the one who worked for his success. In fact, I was at the pub grabbing a bite when I overheard Mike having dinner with Alvin at the bar. They were talking about Dean's business and with him dead, they might be able to pick it up from his family for pennies on the dollar. I'm pretty sure none of the Hartleys would want to move up here and run it."

I wondered why she would say that but held my question, once again employing the tactic of patiently waiting for a person to keep talking. She didn't even seem to notice I hadn't nibbled on that hook before she kept talking.

"Dean didn't have much to do with his family. He never said why, only that they had some kind of falling out."

I nodded and wondered what else she'd say.

"If Mike or Alvin are making plans to pick up the place cheap and turn a quick profit, they have no idea how hard business really is. No one knows more than me how hard Dean worked. I was out at his place all the time, trying to be an extra set of hands. But he insisted on doing it all solo." She made a clucking sound of disapproval. "I hope the police look into Mike's whereabouts when Dean was murdered. No one should have to die like that, with pruners stuck in him and toes pointed to the sky."

Shaking her head, she tapped the books I had given her, and I couldn't help but notice her perfectly manicured nails, but they were a pale-beige color. "I'll take these if you'd ring me up."

"Come over to the counter, and I'll give you a bag too." My mind turned over this new information about Mike and Alvin already planning on taking over the greenhouse operation even before the investigation had finished. I wanted to ask when she overheard the conversation, but that was being too presumptuous, and I didn't want it to look like I was overly interested with her gossip when that's why she had come in—to share this little tidbit of news.

After I finished ringing her up, I said, "Thank you for stopping in today, and I hope you find the books a good resource."

"I'm sure I will." She gave me a wide smile. "You have a good day now, Lily."

I leaned against the counter and watched as she closed the door and crossed the town square. I wasn't sure if I saw a jauntiness to her step or maybe it was all in my imagination, but she had pointed the direction of suspicion at Mike and Alvin. While I was contemplating what Edie had said, the lamps on the desk and side tables near the wingback chairs blinked and they popped, leaving the store in semi-darkness. I hurried into the back room to find replacement bulbs in the cupboard, but the box was gone. I must have forgotten to buy more the last time I replaced them. Grabbing my keys and wallet, I called to Milo that I was running over to Tucker's and would be back in a couple of minutes.

As I approached Tucker's Hardware, Dax was coming from the opposite direction. He gave me a warm smile and jogged to reach the door before I grabbed the door handle, and he opened it for me.

"Hi. Fancy meeting you here." His smile was wide and he was dressed in his usual pressed dark jeans and blue shirt, but today he wasn't wearing the suit jacket but a windbreaker in black. Did the man own anything that had color?

"Hi, Dax. I just had a couple of light bulbs burn out. What are you here for?"

"More than one, huh? That stinks."

I stepped in front of him, and since I knew where Tucker kept an ample supply of light bulbs, I strode down the aisle. I didn't want to leave the bookstore closed for too long since lately I'd been closed more to poke around and learn things, like who might have a motive to kill Dean.

Dax trailed behind me. When I turned to ask him if there was something he needed in this aisle too, I noticed Mike Shaw. He was at the counter purchasing a set of loppers just like the ones that had been the murder weapon. I placed my finger across my lips, hoping Dax would remain quiet so I could hear the interaction between Tucker and

Mike. Dax turned to look at what or who I was concentrating on, and he remained still.

"You need another pair of these already?" Tucker asked.

Mike withdrew his wallet from his back pocket after placing the tool on the counter. "Yeah. I can't find the set I just bought. Darnedest thing. I usually put things back in my shed, but they came up missing." He handed Tucker his credit card. "These just can't be beat. They stay sharp and don't rust."

I wanted to ask him if that's why he used them to kill Dean, but I kept quiet. No sense in blowing my relative cover as I listened and watched.

"You only got the others, what, less than a month ago now?"

Mike gave him a look but never responded to the question. He jammed his card into his wallet and then his pocket without bothering to take the receipt. He glared at Tucker and stormed out the door with loppers in hand.

I glanced at Dax, and he had a look of curiosity on his face that I felt. Had we just seen Mike purchase a replacement for the murder weapon? Grabbing his arm, I pulled Dax toward the back of the store. I looked around, but we were alone.

Dropping my voice, I asked, "I think we just saw a guilty man purchasing garden pruners."

His eyes were locked on mine, and he didn't hesitate to ask, "What do you know?"

I didn't want to tell Dax before I had fully processed what Edie said, and Gage should be the first person I talked to, but in this moment, it seemed like a good idea to spill the details.

"Edie Jenkins came into the store today on the premise she wanted to buy some organic gardening books, but I think she wanted to have the opportunity to gossip. While I was helping her, she mentioned, very casually, that Mike and Alvin were talking about trying to buy Dean's business super cheap. Seems Mike was jealous of Dean's success, and yesterday, when I bumped into Alvin and his sister Ava at the greenhouse, it was easy to tell Alvin was not a fan of Dean's. It seemed it had more to do with his affection for Ava and not his business. But they did want to get into the greenhouse and were upset that Gage had installed a new padlock on the door."

Dax nodded and took in every word, and despite not asking any questions, I could imagine his wheels were turning with ideas. "And you haven't told Gage about your conversation with Ms. Jenkins yet?"

"No. She left the shop just a bit ago and I wanted to get some work done before giving him a call. When Edie and I talked, it was interesting, but in light of what we just witnessed, it takes on a whole new meaning."

"I agree." He checked the area and over his shoulder, he said, "Get your light bulbs and call Gage. He should be brought into the loop right away."

I touched his arm to stop him from striding down the aisle. "Dax, do you think Dean's death has anything to do with the real estate scheme that you've been investigating?" With Mike and Alvin talking about scooping the greenhouse up, worry passed over me like a cold chill on a November morning. There had been too much happening in Pembroke Cove in the last few months. I don't ever remember it being in an upheaval like this before.

Dax stopped his forward motion and came back to where my feet were glued to the old wooden floor. "What's wrong? You've got that crease between your eyes that you get when something is troubling you."

It was interesting that he knew my facial expressions, but he didn't answer my question which added to my worry. Could he think they were tied together and he didn't want to say? "Never mind." I took an oversized box of light bulbs from the shelf and walked toward the counter with him trailing me. After I paid Tucker for the bulbs, I gave him a wink. "Good job chatting up Mike."

He grinned. "Just good customer service."

I pushed the heavy wood and glass door open with Dax still behind me.

Popping one hand on a hip, I said, "Are you going to follow me back to my store?"

He planted his feet wide, hands jammed in his front pockets. "Yes, unless you tell me what is bugging you. I know it's not Dean's case; it's something else."

Throwing my hand up in the air, I exhaled. "Pembroke Cove was a quiet, sleepy little town until Flora dug into things that were better left alone, and it feels like her audacity to line her own pockets has led this town to become a place where neighbors aren't good neighbors, people who you thought were friends want to kill you, and some actually succeed. How did it come to this? And I asked you if there was any way Dean's death was tied to the real estate investigation, and you didn't bother to even answer the question."

Dax opened his mouth and then pointed behind me. "Maybe you should ask Gage."

I twirled around, ready to stomp off, when I noticed Gage was jogging in our direction. And just like that, a calmness wrapped around me and I knew everything was going to be okay. Between the two of us, we could fix anything and that included our small seaside hometown.

Chapter 14
Lily

"Hi." Gage smiled at me and glanced at Dax, a slight frown crossing his brow before it vanished. "I went by the store and saw the closed sign. Is everything okay?"

"Yes. A few light bulbs burned out at the same time, and for some reason, I didn't have any in the cupboard. I bumped into Dax at the hardware store and while we were there, something interesting happened."

Dax said, "Make sure you tell him about Edie Jenkins too."

Gage scanned the area. "We should go back to your store where we can talk in private."

I fell into step with Gage and Dax did the same on my other side. Maintaining a straight face, I said, "Jeez. I hope people don't think you both arrested me."

Dax chuckled and Gage grinned. "I guess it does look like something is going on, but instead of thinking like it's a negative, you can think it's more like we have great taste in friends."

I didn't glance at either of them as I withdrew the key

from my bag to unlock the front door. Without a doubt Milo saw us coming across the town square and he'd linger close by to listen in to our conversation. It would save me from having to repeat myself about the Mike Shaw incident after the guys left.

Gage took the box of bulbs from me and without me asking, he set about replacing them in the darkened lamps. In minutes, the shop was flooded with light.

The tension in the room was awkward, and a hot beverage could do wonders to change that. "Does anyone want coffee? I'm going to fix some."

The men said yes, and I slipped into the back room to escape the palpable stress in the shop. Way too much male territorial shenanigans for my taste. But didn't I kind of set this up with a date with Dax? Even if Gage hadn't made a move, it was obvious he wasn't thrilled with the current situation. Look at me, a witch in the throes of a romantic triangle of sorts. Three is a magical number after all. With a snort of laughter, I set three mugs out, my two favorites, *Booked for the Weekend,* and the other said *Just One More Page.* Gage and I always had our coffee from these, but the third was a basic navy-blue mug. I couldn't conjure up a saying on that one for the occasion. I clasped the black tourmaline and amethyst protection necklace that Aunt Mimi had given me when I first discovered out I was a witch. As usual it was cool to the touch which seemed to indicate no danger on the horizon.

The coffee sputtered into each mug, and I fixed two the way I had many times before, but I hesitated over Dax's. What had he put in his when we met at the Copper Kettle? My mind was blank.

"I take mine black." The sound of Dax's voice made me jump.

I turned to give him a smile. Extending a mug to him, he smiled his thanks.

"I wanted to get to you before you added cream and sugar."

"How did you...?" My voice trailed off when it dawned on me he was a trained observer of behavior and he had seen me drink coffee on many occasions.

He took a step closer, and his dark eyes had softened into pools of black velvet. His voice a deep Southern drawl that I found utterly charming, he said, "There are some things I don't forget, Lily."

My mouth went dry, and relief washed over me as Milo jumped into my arms. Grateful for the interruption, I said, "Hey, little man, where were you hiding?"

He patted my cheek with his paw which I was certain was for show and said, "As your familiar, I also serve as your wingman when necessary."

I knew that Dax and Gage would only hear him meow since only another witch could understand him. Kissing the top of his head, I set him on the floor. "Stay out of mischief, Milo."

He lingered in the doorway and then led the way to the upholstered chairs as I carried coffee mugs for Gage and myself.

"I changed the rest of the bulbs for good measure." He took the coffee I handed to him and bent over to pet Milo. "Ready to tell me what happened around here this morning. It seems I'm the last to know." He gave a sharp look at Dax who didn't even bother to shrug a shoulder. Instead, he dragged the stool from behind the counter to the small seating area.

Once we were settled and had a sip of coffee, I relayed to Gage what had happened with Edie and then told him how we had seen Mike purchasing the same pruners that had been used at Dean's. "But the real kicker was when he didn't answer Tucker's question about what had happened to his." I took another sip. "But more than anything, Gage, it was Mike's demeanor. He was defensive, guarded, and almost resentful of Tucker making casual conversation."

Gage blew on his coffee before he took another sip. "So far I have no significant evidence that Mike was involved other than his bad temper getting the best of him."

Dax asked, "Who are your primary suspects?"

I jumped into the conversation. "Alvin is at the top of the list. With him and Ava trying to get into the greenhouse and he obviously had a short fuse when it came to Dean and Ava dating, he's the most logical suspect. And from what Ava said to me, she was in love with the man. I don't think she could have hurt him."

Gage nodded. "Which leads us back to Alvin. I'm going to bring him in for questioning without Ava. See if I can dig deeper into what he had against Dean. If it was just brotherly concern, that's one thing, but in light of Edie talking about Mike and Alvin wanting to buy the business, that is a motive for murder."

"Money always is," Dax agreed.

"Where do we go from here?" I looked between the two men. "And Dax, you never answered me if you thought this had anything to do with your investigation."

Gage glared at Dax. "Is that what you told Lily?"

He held up his coffee mug in protest. "No. I never said anything about the two crimes being connected. She put two pieces together and came up with five."

"Are you saying these aren't related? It seems like they could be. What's happened so far is related to cheating people out of money for real estate and with Mike's plan to gain control over the greenhouse, it seems to fit perfectly."

Gage nodded. "Like a puzzle piece."

Understanding blanched Dax's face. "I hadn't thought of it in those terms." He grew quiet, and we all drank coffee as the conversation stalled. Finally, he said, "Tell me everything you know about Mike Shaw."

I looked to Gage to see if he wanted to begin. He smiled at me. "I've got this one, but jump in if I miss any of the good stuff."

Smiling at him, I leaned back in my chair. Gage was usually spot-on with details so I doubted there would be much for me to contribute.

"Mike Shaw, mid-fifties. Single. Never been married to my knowledge. He's lived in Pembroke Cove for most of his adult life. I remember him when I was a kid being the man on the street who never gave out candy on Halloween or decorated for the holidays, not even a wreath on his door. He had a reputation for being a surly miser. Kids didn't bother to go to his door selling cookies or calendars from the school fundraisers."

"He was one of those guys who kept to himself too?" Dax asked.

"Not necessarily. He was active in the garden club, and his flower gardens around his house were always stunning. Most of the time he was rude and obnoxious, but he seemed to have some friends in the club."

Dax asked, "What does he do for work?"

Gage said, glancing at me as if for confirmation, "Nothing as far as I can tell. Never has either."

"But he drives a nice truck and his house is pretty nice too, so he must have some sort of income." Gage nodded as I spoke and Dax frowned.

"I'll check into him, but I doubt he's a person of interest for my case, but you never know. Did he ever come up in conjunction with Flora Gray's murder?"

An involuntary shiver raced down my arms as I thought of finding the head librarian on the stone steps of the library.

"Gage, I don't remember anything about him then, do you? He didn't regularly attend movie nights either."

"No." Gage drained the last of his coffee. "I'm going to head back to the police station and ask Alvin Springs to come down and answer a few questions, and maybe for good measure, I'll ask Ava to come down and talk with her separately. That might be just enough to rattle Alvin into shedding light on what's really going on with Dean's business, past and future."

I took Gage's mug and set it on the table in front of us. "What time do you think he'll be in? I want to drop by around the same time."

He gave me his stink eye. "Absolutely not. I don't want you anywhere near this investigation any more than you already have been."

Dax said, "I agree with Gage. Third time is not the charm when it comes to murder. You've gotten lucky so far escaping without injury, but your luck might be running out."

Frankly, I was tired of everyone telling me to stay out of this case, and I couldn't believe what I was hearing. If it wasn't for my observation skills, it would have taken Gage twice as long to get where he was today, and as for Dax, he needed to pay attention to the real estate schemer. The detective and investigator might be smart, but I was the puzzle master, and this was still a grand puzzle to solve.

"Fine. You run along to the police station. I have work to do."

Gage narrowed his eyes. "Lily, remember you promised me you wouldn't go back to the greenhouse alone."

"Who said I was going to?" I stood up. "I have a bookstore to run, and there's that book Aunt Mimi wants me to finish reading." Flashing them both a wide, innocent smile, I said, "I have more than enough to keep myself focused on other things besides your day jobs. And you get paid to solve your mystery; for me it's just a fun hobby."

"There's nothing fun about what has happened around here lately." Gage's voice had a hard edge to it.

Which brought me back to an earlier thought. "Gage, why do you think we've had three people die in the last few months? Our town has always been a safe haven for all who live here."

His smile dimmed. "Lily, there has always been bad things that happen in town which I think you've been oblivious to. Crimes have been committed; people have died unexpectedly, but for some reason, which I can't explain, all of a sudden you're in the center of everything."

Dax's eyes widened. In a teasing voice, he said, "Maybe you're the person behind the current crime wave."

"Dang, I hope that's not the case or I'd have to shut down the store and move to parts unknown." I flashed them both a wide grin. "But I have a lot to do today." I stood up.

Gage and Dax did the same, and I hoped they would take the hint and leave. I had a great idea for the spell I had been working on, and if Milo was right, magic was much more fluid than I had originally thought. But what if my magic had something to do with the crimes? Maybe Dax wasn't as far from the truth as he thought. Now I needed for them to leave. I had to talk to Milo and even call Aunt Mimi. If anyone would understand, it would be her.

Gage bent over and his lips brushed my cheek in his normal fashion. "I'll call you later."

I nodded and looked at Dax's chin. There was no way I was going to look him in the eye after he had witnessed the familiarity between the two of us.

"I'll see you later, Lily." If a confident man's voice could sound defeated, I had just heard it.

"Nice to see you, Dax." The funny thing was, I meant it. He had irritated me when he'd first moved to town, but he had grown on me, and I liked him, as a person, not as a boyfriend. My heart belonged elsewhere.

After the door closed, I sunk in the chair, and Milo trotted over to me, hopping up where Gage had been sitting.

"How does it feel to have not one but two guys vying for your affection?"

"Stop. I had one simple date with Dax, and you know how it's always been with me and Gage."

Milo narrowed his green eyes. "It's time you tell him how you feel. You are a powerful witch, and you need to be brave with Detective Cutie too."

My lower lip jutted out, forming a pout. "I know but—"

He held up a paw, much like a human would hold up his hand to have me stop talking. "Just tell him."

Nodding, I sat up. "Milo, does my finding out I'm a witch have anything to do with people dying? Am I the reason there have been three murders in town?"

He hopped from the chair to my lap and stared deep into my eyes. "Don't even go there. Witches don't cause people to become murderers; however, now you're more in tune with the world around you. Your intuition is keener, and you're listening to your inner voice. Most non-magicals plod along in their own lives, never noticing what is happening around them. If you don't believe me, ask Gage how many people have been murdered in the last year in the county. You'll discover it is more than the three in our sleepy little town."

I wanted to believe what he said so I chose to. Pulling Milo into my arms, I showered him with kisses before I set him on the floor. "In that case, I have an idea for the disappearing spell. So let's get to work. I think you're right about the book. It gives me what I need when I need it, and this one might come in handy before whoever is responsible for killing Dean is arrested."

Chapter 15
Gage

As I watched Alvin and Ava walk out of the police station, I looked down the sidewalk and street. I had half expected Lily to just happen to saunter into the police station after the brother and sister arrived, but she hadn't. Maybe she was finally starting to realize I was good at my job and if she needed to know something, and I could tell her, I would. With a snort, I walked back in my office. Not likely.

Dax was sitting in the visitor chair and glanced up from his phone as I sat down. "What did you think of the interviews?"

Without hesitation, I replied, "They're both hiding something, but I'm starting to like Ava for the murder. Crime of passion."

"Why? She seems like she was really in love with Dean and broken up over his death."

I leaned back in my chair. "She started to say something about another woman, but then clammed up. As if she suspected him of not being exclusive with her."

Dax crossed one leg over the other and folded his hands

in his lap, a sure sign this conversation was going to last longer than I originally thought. Now that the Springs were gone, I wanted to get over to Lily's and see what she might think of Dean dating other women.

"Maybe Dean never stated he was only seeing Ava. It's not uncommon for people to date several people at one time."

I didn't like where this was going. Was he talking about the case or was he beginning to tread into my relationship with Lily? "Usually if people are dating others, both parties agree." I did my best to keep my voice flat, but the way Dax's nostrils flared, I guessed we had moved from the case to the woman I cared about.

He leaned forward. "What's the story between you and Lily? You're friends, I get that, but there's this vibe that you're sending out, and if you're into her more than friends, you should tell her and make it official. Otherwise, people get the wrong idea that they might stand a chance with her."

I did not want to have this conversation with Dax Peters. My office phone buzzed, and I picked it up.

"Peabody?"

"Detective, Nikki Twing is here with a very large dog. She said she needs to see you right away. It might have something to do with the case."

What could Nikki need to see me about? There was only one way to find out, and it would get me out of this conversation with Dax too. "Tell her I'll be right out." I hung up and pushed back my chair. "I need to go."

Dax stood. "I have things to do. I'm going to see if there's a connection between Mike Shaw and my case. If there is anything relevant, I'll let you know."

I extended my hand. No need for things to be awkward

between us. As law enforcement officers, ultimately, we were on the same side of the fence. "I appreciate that."

Nikki was holding a leash for the largest Great Dane I had ever seen. But the dog seemed to be mesmerized by the woman. He was sitting at her feet staring at her with adoration. It was easy to see the dog had bonded with her.

"Gage." Her eyes lit up and an easy smile spread over her face as I walked across the lobby. "I'm sorry to drop by, but I thought you might need to talk to me about something." She glanced at Dax and said hello, but with much less enthusiasm. If there were sides to take, she had made it clear she was on team Gage.

"Nikki." Dax greeted her as he walked past and out the glass door.

"Let's go in the conference room, and you can tell me what brought you here." I pushed open the door and held it wide for her and the dog. "If I didn't know any better, I'd swear you knew I could use a distraction. The conversation with Dax was going places I didn't want it to."

"No need to thank me. I'm just glad I showed up when I did." She touched the dog's shoulder which came to her hip, and he sat down without so much as a bark.

"That is one well-trained dog." I scratched between his ears and the dog turned to look at Nikki, as if asking her for approval.

"It's okay, Brutus. Gage is a good friend."

She unclipped his collar and handed it to me. "Look at this and tell me what you think?"

Taking the wide leather band, I noticed the dog's neck had a red mark. "It looks as if this has been rubbing the poor fella's skin."

Nikki pulled out a small pot from her pocket and opened it. "Salve to help it heal. Take a closer look at the collar. There's something inside of it." She rubbed the salve on the pup's neck, and I turned the leather collar over in my hands. She was right; there was a distinct lump.

I pulled a small knife from my pocket and separated the leather, which under the blade gave way easily. A key fell out into the palm of my hand. I held it up. "I wonder what this goes to?"

Brutus moaned a little, and he had Nikki's full attention before she said, "I would guess a lockbox that Dean kept in the house."

I pursed my lips as I thought back to the search of the house and the items we had tagged as evidence. But nothing that could use a key like this sprang to mind.

With a slight shrug, she suggested, "Maybe under a floorboard, like in a closet?"

I gave her a sharp look. "Why would you say that?"

With a wide-eyed innocent look, she said, "That's where I'd hide something that was very important, so not just anyone could find it."

Brutus rested his head on my leg and looked up at me with such sad eyes it prompted me to ask, "What's going to happen to him?"

"I'm fostering him for now, but if I can't find him a home, I'll have to post his picture and information on one of those pet finder places and I'm sure he'll be adopted. He might even get a plane ride out of it."

"What? He could be adopted by just anyone?" The idea this sweet pup would have to find a new family and heaven only knew where, didn't sit well with me. "What if someone in town wanted to adopt him?"

"So far no one has come forward, and I can't keep him

forever. Murphy has been good with him, but my house is kind of a one dog home, so..." Nikki looked at me with her big baby blues, and that was it. As if under her spell, I said, "What if I adopt him?" I couldn't believe those words came out of my mouth.

Her smile grew. "That is a fantastic idea. I'm not sure why I didn't think of that before we came over today."

The dog slid from her side to mine, and I was pretty sure this big lug of a dog had claimed me as his person.

She handed me his leash and laughed softly. "Obviously, Brutus has made his decision too. Congratulations and you're in luck. He can go home with you tonight. I just came from the store and I have a fifty-pound bag of kibble in my car. You can toss it in your truck, and I'm sure you two will settle in tonight like cake and frosting."

"I was going to swing by Lily's on my way home. How about you take him, and I'll pick Brutus up after. I wouldn't want to upset Milo. The whole cat and dog rivalry thing."

Nikki waved her hand as if she were batting away a fly. "You have nothing to worry about. Milo is great with dogs."

I wasn't so sure, but I'd soon find out. "I'll shoot Lily a text and let her know I have a new sidekick."

"First, help me load his stuff into your truck. I have a cake order that I need to finish and deliver tonight."

Following her outside, holding Brutus's leash was not something I thought I'd be doing when I woke up this morning, but here I was, a dog dad.

She opened the hatch on her vehicle and said, "You can drop the leash. Trust me, he won't go anywhere. He's going to keep a close eye on his kibble and on you."

After the transfer was made, I opened the passenger door and before I could encourage him to get inside, Brutus hopped in like we had been doing this for years instead of our first time. Maybe Dean used to take him for rides in his truck. And so far, Nikki was right; the dog was very well mannered.

"Say hi to Lily for me." She got in her SUV and waved as she drove away.

Before I closed the door, I withdrew my phone and took a picture of Brutus sitting in the passenger seat looking around and then forwarded it to Lily. "Guess who I'm bringing with me?" The whoosh sound confirmed the image had been sent and I patted his head. "Ready, boy?"

With a soft woof that I decided served as a yes, I shut the door and climbed in on my side. My phone pinged with an incoming text.

This is a surprise. Can't wait to hear all about it. See you soon.

She just rolled with whatever came her way. I knew why Dax wanted to date her; she was one in a million.

When I arrived at Lily's, she was standing on her back deck waiting for me, or I should say us. As soon as Brutus saw her, he gave a deep woof and began to wiggle excitedly. "Hey, boy, do you remember her?" I stroked the top of his head, and he woofed again. Reaching around him, I pushed open the door so he could get out and pad the short distance to her. The dog had great taste in women.

Kneeling, Lily wrapped her arms around the dog's neck and kissed the top of his head. He lapped up the attention like a puppy, and I can't say I blamed him. "Hello there, you big baby." She looked up at me, and by the sparkle in her eyes, I knew she was happy to see me as well as the dog. "How did this come about?" She picked up the leash that was lying on the ground and opened the back door. "Come in and tell me everything."

The comment had more meaning than just about my impulsive dog adoption. But to be fair, she had discovered new information about Mike Shaw, and in return I would fill her in on some of the highlights of my conversation with Alvin and Ava.

The smell of chicken roasting teased my senses as I entered the cozy kitchen. The table was set for two, with a squat bouquet of fall-colored flowers and even beeswax candles. My heart dipped. We hadn't talked about dinner so she must have plans with Dax.

Lily opened a cupboard and pulled out a box of small dog biscuits and gave a couple to Brutus who very gently took them in his mouth and went to lay down by the door. She grinned at Gage. "I keep a box around for Murphy."

At the mention of Nikki's dog, it all made sense, and I should have guessed; she wasn't clairvoyant. "Thank you." I nodded in the direction of the table. "I won't keep you long. I just wanted to fill you in on my conversations with the Springs." A frown flashed over her face, and I guessed I should have called first.

"I'm making dinner for us."

"Oh." I could feel heat rise in my cheeks. "Sorry. Since you and Dax had a date, I just assumed that..." My voice died when I realized the candles and flowers were for us. Hope sprang in my chest. "Dinner smells delicious."

She held out her hand, and I took it as she guided me into the living room. "Have a seat on the couch." Lily waited until I sat down before sitting next to me. She was chewing on the corner of her lip when she lifted her eyes to meet mine. "We need to talk."

I nodded, my heart hammering in my chest. "Okay, what do you want to talk about?"

"Us." Her voice was true and clear, and the word seemed to hang in the air.

I waited for her to continue since I hoped I knew where it was headed but I wasn't sure.

Clasping her hands together on her lap, she said, "I had coffee with Dax."

My heart sank. This might not be going in the direction I had hoped. But I wasn't about to jump to conclusions; instead, I was going to give her time to speak her mind.

"But the entire time I was with him, I wished you were sitting across from me." She took my hand and gave it a squeeze. "Gage, I have been in love with you most of my life, and if I don't tell you, I'm worried we're going to be like Aunt Mimi and Nate. I'll spend the rest of my days wishing we were together, and if I don't tell you how I feel, then nothing will change. If you don't feel the same way about me, I understand, but I needed to be honest with you."

The air whooshed from my lungs, and I drew Lily into my arms. "I've loved you my entire life, and if you're ready to try dating me, then I'm all in." I wanted her to say yes.

"Gage. You really feel the same way!"

Chuckling, I said, "Yes. And I'm so happy that one of us was brave enough to finally admit it."

Lily pulled out of my arms and grinned. "You've made me so happy. But there's just one more thing."

My heart dipped again. I didn't think my ticker could take the constant highs and lows tonight. "You can tell me anything."

"We can't start a relationship until you know the full truth about who and what I am." Her eyes never broke our connection. "I'm a witch."

Chapter 16
Lily

The look on Gage's face when I announced I was a witch was absolutely priceless, disbelief and relief combined into one expression. "I'm sure this must come as a shock; it did to me too when I learned the truth. Aunt Mimi and Nikki are both witches along with my dad, but Mom isn't."

Gage started to laugh. "You're sure? Like do you have a broom and everything?"

"Of course, well, not the broom, at least not yet." I narrowed my eyes and gave him my best annoyed look. "Why are you laughing so hard?"

"You're never going to believe this, but my mother is a witch."

I knew my eyes grew round as saucers, but he quickly said, "But I'm not magical." He wiped the tears from the corners of his eyes from laughing so hard.

It was my turn to be surprised. "Your mom is a witch? Right here in Pembroke Cove?" I got up and walked to the front window. Why hadn't Aunt Mimi or Nikki told me?

"I only have one mom so yes, and you can imagine I was

disappointed when I discovered I wasn't. That's why I became a police officer. There have been some occasions when her visions have helped me." His eyes widened. "At the library, you wrapped me in a protection spell to save me? And the sign, you got it off me?"

I couldn't contain my smile. "Yup, and you bet I did."

"And when you were on the widow's walk in the storm, you were able to get the broom to fly? It wasn't the wind?"

"Right again." When Gage mentioned that spell, I realized in a stressful situation I could easily call up my magic and save myself. Milo was right; I wasn't a half-bad witch after all.

"How long have you known, like for years? Is that why you're so good with puzzles? You're clairvoyant or something?"

"You probably don't remember when I got hit on the head with a book at my store, the same day as Flora died? After I was done seeing stars, Milo announced that he was my familiar and I was a witch. The book that clonked me on the head was my textbook to learn everything I could about witchcraft. So, basically, that sums up my last few months."

His mouth dropped open and then snapped shut before he asked, "Milo can talk?"

"Yes, and he does all the time." I tipped my head from side to side. "He can be a bit snarky and don't tell him I said this"—I looked at the doorway before continuing—"but he's usually right."

The timer went off on the stove, and I needed to check on dinner, but I didn't want to leave all of this up in the air, especially if Gage had questions. And I had a few lingering thoughts about his mom too.

He got up from the couch and shook his head as if clearing cobwebs from his brain. "Why don't we have dinner while I digest all this new information, and if you're interested or want to, we can talk about the case."

What did he mean by that? Of course we were going to talk about the case. But I wasn't about to pounce on him for details about Alvin and Ava, even if I wanted to. The bigger question in the room was our potential relationship status which he hadn't even said a word about after I confessed to my witch status. Yet.

Brutus lifted his head and laid it back down, completely unfazed at what might be happening. Milo was nowhere to be seen which didn't surprise me either. Together we got dinner on the table and sat down.

Gage stretched his hand across the table and wiggled his fingers. I placed my hand in the palm of his and his long fingers entwined with mine. "Before we talk about anything else, I want you to rewind to when you said you were in love with me. What made you finally tell me?"

I smiled and squeezed his hand. "You mean other than the fact that I might have gotten impatient waiting for you to say something?"

He chuckled. "You're right; I should have spoken up years ago." Gage slid his chair around the kitchen table and placed his arm around my back. "In my job, I must be strong and brave and face whatever comes my way head-on, but with you, I wasn't willing to take the chance and risk losing our friendship. I told myself it was better to have you in my life as a friend even if you didn't feel the same way. Even when William told me he could see how I felt about you and that I needed to stop wasting time and tell you, I just couldn't."

I turned in my seat so I could look him in the eye. "Wait, William, as in the Sweet Spot, knew?"

He nodded. "Yup, said it was easy to see that I was a man in love."

Curious, I asked, "When was that and why didn't you speak up?"

"It was after the Clam Bake sign crashed down on me. I guess he figured that should be a wake-up call that anything can happen. But I was still content; I didn't want to rock the boat."

"And here I come along and do just that."

"My personal hurricane," he said.

"No, I can't control the weather. I'm a beginner witch, and most of my spells are haphazard at best."

"I would disagree with that, considering your success so far." Laughing, he brushed a lock of hair behind my ear and gave me the most loving look I had ever seen. "What kind of a witch are you?"

"I'm more of a generalist. Not like Nikki who's a kitchen witch, or Aunt Mimi who's a cosmic witch. She thinks I'm an eclectic witch. Spells will find me as I need them, but so far, unfortunately for you, the kitchen witch side hasn't come out."

He glanced at dinner on the table. "I don't know about that; you can cook a mean roast chicken."

I could feel a flush heat my cheeks. "Enough about the witch stuff. I really want to know about your interviews this afternoon. Did you learn anything that can narrow the scope of our investigation?"

Gage didn't reposition his chair but stayed close to me. I could get used to this for sure. "After talking with the Springs, my gut is telling me Alvin is the most likely suspect, not Ava. There was no respect for Dean's business practices but more than that, Alvin hated that Ava was dating him. The venom in his voice and the fierce look on his face made my blood run cold. I've never seen anyone with so much restrained rage directed at another. But Ava is still a possibility since she insinuated there might have been another woman in Dean's life, a rival."

I thought about bumping into the brother and sister at Dean's and there was anger, and Alvin hadn't attempted to disguise it. "But the way Dean was killed was more like an accident, not in a fit of rage. If Alvin had been the killer, wouldn't he have done it in a different way? Maybe poison? There are all those herbicides in the greenhouse. I'm sure something in there would have done the trick."

"Poisons are typically a woman's choice of murder. Men usually go for more physical ways for someone to die. If it had been poison, I'd be zeroing in on Ava for sure, but with her being petite, she might not have the strength to use the garden shears unless she was very angry and adrenaline kicked in."

I didn't want to think I had once again been in close proximity to a murderer, and knowing I had been mere feet from Alvin made my blood turn to ice. "Do you think he'd hurt Ava?"

He touched my cheek. "No, and Alvin would never have hurt you with Nikki and his sister right there. But this is why I don't want you to go off by yourself to the greenhouse. Until Alvin is arrested, it's too dangerous."

Nodding, I said, "I promise until he's behind bars, I won't go anywhere near that place."

"Good. Now, can we eat? I'm starving and kitchen witch or not, this dinner has smelled amazing from the moment I walked in the door."

Tipping my head, I said, "One more question."

He just grinned. "Isn't there usually just one more?"

"When are you going to arrest Alvin?"

"Tomorrow morning. I have a couple of minor details to check out, and as long as there are no surprises, he'll be in handcuffs by ten."

I exhaled a long sigh of relief. It was almost over. Dean's murderer would be behind bars tomorrow, and this time, I hadn't gotten into anything where I was over my head, but I had helped solve the mystery.

After dinner Gage and I reclined on the sofa, shoulder to shoulder and our hands clasped and fingers intertwined. He said, "When Nikki was at the station with Brutus, she put some salve on his neck. His collar was rubbing, and when I took a good look at it, I discovered a key. It seems Dean left it for someone to find."

I had been feeling relaxed, but now I sat straight up. He had my full attention. "Really? What does it go to?"

"I'm going to take a run out to the house tomorrow with Peabody and Mac. Care to join us, if you promise not to touch anything?"

This was the first time he had suggested I tag along while he was actively investigating, not as a follow-up visit.

Tapping the end of my nose with his index finger, he said, "Don't think this will be our new normal, but by the time we go, Alvin will be in jail and you're safe with me."

I couldn't help but grin from ear to ear. "You do know I have a few skills that you don't to help protect myself, and it will help us in finding whatever the key goes to as well."

He gave me a side-eyed look. "Didn't you confess before that you need to work on your spells?"

"What I really said was I'm a new witch and have some catching up to do." I leaned back against the couch cushions. "Tell me about your mother and how long have you known she was a witch and what kind is she?"

"Three questions rolled into one sentence." Draping his arm around my shoulders, he held me close. "I've always known; it's just a part of who she is. I didn't realize until I went to school that not everyone's mom was a witch. The first day of kindergarten I came home and told Mom about some kid whose mother couldn't stir a pot with a wave of her hand or brew teas to take away a stomachache." He smiled as he seemed to recall the memory. "That's when she sat me down and explained that most people don't believe that witches exist and because of that I shouldn't talk about what she could do. It needed to be a family secret that we could always talk about at home, but I shouldn't tell other children, so I didn't."

"She's a healer?"

He nodded. "She is, and I think a bit of a kitchen witch in general. And I don't have a lick in my body at all. I take after Dad's side of the family, completely non-magical."

"That's like my mom, but she has a gift for blending teas. I inherited my magic from Dad. It took a long while for me to open the book that my aunt gave me. It seems I needed to do that before my powers would kick in, so like I said, I'm late to the coven which, of course, consists of Mimi, Nikki, and me at this point. I don't know how many witches live in Pembroke Cove. A part of me is curious, but the other part doesn't want to ask too many questions." I snapped my fingers. "William knows about me though."

"He does? How?" I watched as Gage's eyes grew larger. "The sign. You used magic to lift it and William pulled me to safety."

"That's right, but I haven't told anyone else. I get where

your mom was coming from and the less people who know until I'm comfortable with my new skills, the better."

He pulled me closer and kissed the side of my head. "Your secret is safe with me, and if you like, we can stop by my parents' at some point and you can talk with my mom about witchcraft. I'm sure she'd love to help you if you wanted it."

"I appreciate that, and I might take you up on it, but for now I'm just"—I did air quotes—"*reading the book.*"

"Why did you say it like it's a fate worse than walking on the beach over broken seashells?"

I sighed. "Every time I have a problem and ask Milo or Aunt Mimi for help, they say, *read the book.*" I groaned. "Then the darn book has a mind of its own and some spells are easy to work and others are so hard. Milo said it's because I'm behind and the book is giving me what I need to master to be ready for what's coming next."

"That's a pretty smart book and I'm glad, it has a mind of its own. After all, if it didn't, you might not have been able to get the sign off me as quickly as you did and who knows how extensive my injuries might have been."

"True." Milo had said almost the exact same thing.

"What are you practicing now?"

As if on cue, Milo strolled into the room and glanced from me to Gage. "Detective Cutie knows our secret?"

"He does." I smiled at Gage. "Turns out his mother is a witch too."

"Tell me something I don't know, Ms. Witch."

"Why didn't you tell me?" I crossed my arms over my chest, and Gage's head was cocked as if he were trying to understand our conversation. Thankfully, he didn't interrupt.

"I'm not going to out a witch to a brand-new witch. It's

just not done." With a swish of his long gray tail, Milo stalked from the room without a backward glance but paused in the doorway. "For the record, I like the dog. Not much of a talker yet, but he'll get used to me, and you need to practice your new spell, so the boyfriend needs to leave." Then Milo was gone.

"What was that all about?" Gage asked.

"He likes Brutus, and he wasn't about to tell me that your mother was a witch which means if he knows of others, he won't tell me."

"He seemed to talk for longer than that."

I gave him a sidelong look before answering. "Once again, he reminded me to get back to practicing my spells."

"What does he know that he's not telling you? And what spell are you working on?"

My shoulders drooped when I thought of how miserably I was failing at the spell. "I need to learn how to make an object disappear."

He got up from the couch and pulled me to my feet. Sliding his arms around my waist, he held me close enough to be romantic. "Then I'm going home so you can practice. But before I go, would you like to go out to dinner with me on Friday night? We can get dressed up and drive down to Portland? I'd like for our first official date to be very special."

"I would like that very much, but let's make it Saturday. That way I don't need to get up early and go to work the next morning."

He leaned in and my heart quickened as I thought he was going to kiss me on the lips, but instead he kissed my cheek. "That sounds like a perfect idea. I'm already looking forward to it." Our first official date. "I can't wait until Saturday."

"Me too. First, I'll call you in the morning so we can set a time to meet at Dean's. Is that okay?"

"Sounds like a plan."

He kissed my cheek one more time and whistled for Brutus. "Come on, boy. Let's go home."

As I watched Gage and his new best bud get into his truck, happiness slid over me. I couldn't believe after all this time we were dating.

"Excuse me." Milo hopped on the kitchen table. His deep gravelly voice broke my focus. "Now, can we get back to your lesson?"

"Are you always going to be tough on me?"

He began to wash his front paw, pausing long enough to glare at me from his deep-green eyes. "Trust me, you do not want to have a familiar who's a pushover, and you were lucky I chose you."

Waving a finger in the air to protest, I said, "Wait just a minute. I chose you from the shelter."

"And why do you think I was at the Pembroke Cove shelter?" He jabbed a paw in the direction of my book *Practical Beginnings.*

I held up my hands in surrender. "I know. Read the book."

Chapter 17
Lily

Later that night, I closed the spell book, weary from my attempts to perfect the disappearing incantation. I sank into a ladder-back chair and stretched my legs out in front of me. Cramps finally eased in my calves from the endless hours of standing at the counter. What if Milo was right and I should just make up my own spell? The art of the craft was about the intent, not the actual words. I tipped back my head and closed my eyes, wondering what would make for a catchy little spell to cause something to disappear.

I banish the, insert object here, which is, insert location here. I vanish the, insert object here, into thin air. So, banish and vanish I do decree, and so it shall be.

I laughed out loud as I added the insert object and location here, like this could be a mix and match spell. But would it work? Sitting up straight with eyes wide, I looked around the room. If I made something vanish, I needed to be prepared that it was gone since I didn't know how to bring it back. At least not yet. There was a cooking magazine on the counter, ready to be recycled. It didn't matter what happened to that. I stood and concentrated on the glossy cover. In a steady and clear voice, I said, "I banish the magazine from the counter. With a snap of my fingers, it will disappear into thin air. So, banish and vanish I do degree, and so it shall be." With a blink of my eyes and a snap, it was no longer on the counter. I hurried over, opening drawers and cabinets to see if it was there, but clearly it was gone.

A gravelly voice belonging to my sleepy familiar from behind me said, "Now that's what I call a well-executed vanishing spell. But the words aren't typical."

I whirled on my heel and grinned at my gray tabby. "I couldn't do it the way it was written. I couldn't make water disappear in the desert with what the book said, so I made this up. Not exactly a good rhyme but does that matter if it works?"

Milo bent his head in agreement. At least he seemed pleased that I had worked on the spell. "Any idea how to bring it back?"

I grinned. "Nope and that's not for tonight. Tomorrow is another day, and if I get lucky, maybe the book will show me a spell that actually works to bring it back." I flicked off the light switch and sailed past Milo to my bedroom. "Good night, Milo."

"Good night, my dear witch."

I couldn't contain my happiness. When he said that phrase, I knew his words were laced with pride. Within seconds, I fell into a dreamless sleep.

The next morning, I was groggy, and there wasn't enough coffee to wake my brain cells, but after a hot shower and a third cup, the fog was starting to lift. Milo was sitting by the back door when I was ready to leave for work.

"Hello, Milo. Did you sleep well last night?" I scooped him up and placed a light kiss on the top of his soft head.

"By the looks of the bags under your eyes, better than you." He jabbed a paw in the direction of *Practical Beginnings*. "I'm sure there is a spell to take care of the problem."

Groaning, I said, "Milo. I don't have time to learn the spells I'm supposed to, let alone try to make potion lotions. I'll call Aunt Mimi. I'm sure she has something to help me. Besides, I want to tell her that I have a dinner date for Saturday night with a certain detective."

"Other than sharing your long overdue news, what else is planned for today? Are you going out to the scene of the murder again?"

"Yes, with Gage, so I will be perfectly safe." It was nice that Milo worried about me, but in this case, it wasn't necessary. "Are you riding to the store with me this morning or are you taking the long route?" He often met me there, saying he wanted to catch up with the other familiars in town. Not that he told me who they were or who their witches are. Apparently, that was top secret. But eventually I'd find out.

He didn't answer, so I tried a new tactic. Leaning against the counter, trying to come off as super casual, I asked, "Why didn't you tell me about Gage's mother?"

"He finally told you and the rest you'll learn in time."

It was not the response I was hoping for. "Well, until last night, we had never even talked about me being a witch so why would he open up."

"I thought after the festival he'd offer it up, drop it into a conversation like hey, my mother can read tea leaves, or something to that effect."

"Maybe I should stop by and ask her about all the things I saw when I was reading them." I said it more to myself than to Milo.

"Nope. Poor etiquette on your part as a witch. Until other witches are ready to approach you and welcome you into the coven, the best thing to do is wait or if Gage takes you, that's fine. The community is welcoming, but don't get pushy."

My shoulders slumped. Just when I had a new outlet for information it was taken away, but I could be patient. Especially when it came to Gage's mom. "Okay. I'll wait, but it's going to be hard."

"Focus on poking around Dean's house. That should keep you occupied for the day."

He was right about that. No telling what we might find in the mysterious locked box. "Alright then, I will see you later." I gathered up my bags and gave him one last kiss on the head before closing the kitchen door behind me.

"Hey," Milo grumbled as he came out the kitty door. "You could have waited for me."

"I'm sorry, but that's why you have your very own entrance—so you can come and go as you please—and you've rarely ridden to work with me in the last few weeks."

"I've been prowling for clues to help you solve this murder before you find yourself in another life-or-death circumstance."

The monotone statement reminded me that Milo did care about me and we were a bonded pair for life—well, at least for as long as I was alive. My plan was to live to be a very old witch too. "I'm sorry, but Gage said he's going to arrest Alvin today. I thought you heard us talking last night." I scooped him up and gave him a hug. "I appreciate you're concerned about me."

In his gruff way, he said, "It's part of the job."

I kissed him on the top of his head and carried him to the car. He couldn't fool me. Caring was not part of the job; teaching me was.

From the moment I walked into the bookstore, it seemed one thing after another had gone wrong. The coffee pot wouldn't work, and I didn't know a spell to fix it, so after flipping through my book, *Practical Beginnings*, I finally found one. After drinking two cups and caffeine was surging through me, I discovered more light bulbs in the storeroom had burned out and needed to be replaced. This time I had plenty in stock. I thought about calling the electrician but decided that could wait until tomorrow, and then a crash from the back of the store had me hurrying to check that out. Books were scattered all over the floor. Why they had fallen from the shelves was perplexing, and after a close inspection, I could see the shelf wasn't broken. When I tried to pick them up, they wouldn't budge. It was as if each book weighed as much as an elephant.

At the top of my lungs, I yelled, "*Milo!*"

The shop was still. I twirled around and went in search of my familiar and my book of spells. Since magic had brought them to the floor, magic needed to clean up the mess. And if I didn't get things running smoothly, there was no way I could meet Gage at Dean's house to look for the box that fit the mystery key.

My familiar was stretched out in the window seat, gently snoring. "Milo." My voice was razor-sharp.

His tail twitched, but he didn't open his eyes. Grumbling, he said, "You're interrupting my nap."

"Why did you knock all the books off the shelf and cause light bulbs to burn out and break the coffee maker?"

Now he opened one eye and glared at me. "First off, your tone is unnecessary and second, have you ever known me to be able to cast a spell?"

He had me there. I sank down next to him on the window seat. "If you didn't do any of that, then how did it happen?"

He sat up. "This is the second time the bulbs burned out so maybe you need an electrician. This building is ancient, and the coffee pot has been here forever; maybe it's just old."

He had me on those two points. "And the books?"

Before he could answer, the front door burst open and Edie sailed in. "Good morning, Lily." She came over to where we were seated and patted the top of Milo's head.

He grumbled, "Don't be so rough, lady."

She frowned. I glanced at him, and then back at Edie. Getting up from the cushion, I said, "How can I help you today?"

She gave me a bright smile. "I wanted to thank you for the excellent books on gardening when I was in a couple of days ago."

It seemed like it had been weeks, but she was right; it was only a few days. "I'm glad you enjoyed them. Is there anything else I can help you with?"

"No." She glanced around the space as if looking to see if there were other customers before she dropped her voice. "I was wondering if you've heard any news about the investigation." With a wink she said, "I know you and Gage are quite friendly."

I forced a smile to my face instead of the frown that

wanted to appear. "I believe they're very close to an arrest, but I can't say anything more."

Nodding, she walked in the direction of the aisle where the books were on the floor as if she was drawn in that direction. I wanted to stop her, but she said, "I'm just going to browse for a bit if that's okay."

"Of course. I have some work to do." How did I cut her off from seeing the mess? But my mind was a blank. The bell on the door chimed before I could intercept her. Dang. What else could happen this morning?

Aunt Mimi's distinct hello rang out as if she was everywhere at the same time. Edie's steps slowed, and she said, "I'll come back later if that's okay?"

"Certainly, but I'll be out for a while later this morning." I wasn't about to tell her that I was meeting Gage at Dean's place after the arrest.

Edie quirked a brow in question but thankfully never articulated what was on her mind. "I'm sure I'll see you soon." She did an about-face and strode out the door, barely acknowledging my aunt as they passed each other.

Relief coursed through me. Now I could get the books back in place and see what Aunt Mimi thought about all that was happening to me today. She and Milo came toward me as I stood in the middle of a long row of books. Giving her a half-hearted smile, I said, "I'm happy to see you."

"Oh, Lily, I got a strong sense you needed me this morning. What is going on?"

"Broken coffee pots, burned out lights, and an entire shelf of books on the floor, which I can't pick up." She wrapped her arms around me and held on tight. "The first two can be normal, but the books... Aunt Mimi, it has to be magic that they're on the floor."

She released me and gave me a long look before nodding. "There is magic in here, and it's not yours. But there is a spell in your book that will ward off any other witch casting spells in your space. You need to learn it, but first you need to get those books back where they belong." With a squeeze to my hands, she said, "And I can help."

"But how do I do that?" A knot was in my midsection as I was feeling out of my element.

"You can levitate anything. You did it with the Clam Bake sign and once you get the books off the ground, you redirect them like I do with plates. You'll say the incantation and then with intention to get them back on the shelf."

Hope sprang inside me. That was easy. "I can do that if you want to fix the coffee pot?"

Her laugh was musical. "Deal."

We went in different directions, each focused on our own task. I stood in front of the pile of books and closed my eyes. Concentrating on the books, I said softly, *These books are weightless and chainless and now can hover until they slide back in place. This is my wish, so shall it be.* With my hands outstretched, I turned them palms up and moved them in the direction of the shelf. The books floated in midair for a moment before I focused harder on the shelves, and then instantly they clattered back where they belonged. I let out a loud whoop of joy.

I brushed my hands off as if they might be dusty and marveled at how easily the spell had worked. Maybe I was getting the hang of this after all. My cell pinged with an incoming text. Gage had written, *Alvin turned himself in. Proclaims he was in it alone. Doubtful. Meet me at Dean's at two.*

Well, that took care of the arrest. All that was left to do was look for the mysterious box, and I could wait until this afternoon. I shot a quick text back. *See you then.* I went to have coffee with Aunt Mimi. I needed to know more about protecting my bookstore from unwanted witchcraft and the critical question—who was the witch who cast the spell and why?

Chapter 18
Gage

I didn't like putting off looking for the lockbox at Dean's, and it was a great reason to see Lily. But Alvin coming in to surrender wasn't something I had expected at the start of my day. What I hadn't told Lily when I sent her a quick text was that Ava was an hour behind Alvin and she confessed to killing Dean. Two confessions in one morning, and it was obvious they were each trying to protect the other from what they thought might have happened. Sadly, it only muddled the investigation for me.

A sharp rap on my door drew my attention. I looked up and Dax was hovering in the doorway. "Morning."

"Got a minute? I'd like to run something by you."

His timing was perfect. I could use someone to bounce my investigation off too. "Have a seat."

He sat in the chair across from my desk. "How's the investigation going?"

I leaned back, still processing what had already happened. "We'll get to that, but first tell me what's on your mind?"

"My case has gone cold, and I'm just wondering if you've heard of any real estate business being questionable in surrounding towns. With your connections, I thought if you hadn't heard anything, maybe you could make a few calls."

"Yeah, I can do that for you, and it's a good idea. There's no way whoever is behind the money evaporated. They have too much tied up in Pembroke Cove already."

"My thoughts exactly."

Dax crossed one ankle over his other knee. He seemed to be settling in for a longer conversation which had become part of his MO. I wanted to ask him how his date had gone with Lily, just to make sure he didn't have any lingering feelings. Would it be rude to let it slip that we had a dinner date planned for Saturday? But if the shoe was on the other foot, I wouldn't want him rubbing my nose in my loss, so I let that thought go.

"How's your case?" he asked casually, but I could see the gleam of interest lingering in his dark eyes.

"I had two people confess this morning, the Springs, brother and sister."

He never flinched, even if he found it surprising. "Were you expecting that?"

"I had planned to arrest Alvin today, but he beat me to it, and then Ava strolled in and announced she had accidently killed Dean when he fell on the hedge pruners and she panicked, didn't call for help. I think she's hoping to throw herself on the mercy of a judge to avoid anything more than involuntary manslaughter. At least that was the charge she recited to me."

"Not typical for a suspect to name the actual charge that should be against them." Dax grinned. "So where do you go from here?"

I pointed to my whiteboard that had facts listed along with photos of the crime scene. "Back to the beginning since there is no way it's either of them after I questioned them regarding the security footage of the greenhouse."

He sat up straighter in the chair. "What footage?"

"Lily found a USB drive and it had pictures of Dean's security cameras on it, images of him working in the greenhouse. But when I questioned Alvin and Ava separately, they said files got stored on floppy discs."

He broke out in a laugh. "And you bought that?"

I shrugged. "If you don't use computers for anything other than social media and checking your bank statement, why would you need to know technology has changed or use a USB drive."

Dax quirked a brow in disbelief. "You really think neither of them know how to use one?"

"I wasn't sure at first so I did a little test. I handed them each a blank USB and asked them to help me out and open the file on the drive and identify the people who were recorded coming and going from the fall festival."

He nodded and smiled his approval. "Good idea, keep it totally away from the greenhouse images but still see what they each knew."

"Exactly and I was shocked when Ava didn't even know to push the slide button to insert the drive and Alvin couldn't find the slot anywhere on the spare laptop to insert it after he finally figured out how to expose the end." I was confident they hadn't been faking based on sitting quietly while they each struggled, but Dax was bound to go in that direction. Before he did, I said, "I used my normal overly patient tactic and sat while they tried to insert the drive. Ava started using language I never thought I'd hear from her mouth, and Alvin banged the tabletop in frustration. But it was their eyes that gave them away. In my estimation, they were convinced whatever pictures were on that drive might help them wiggle out of their confession, and Ava said that whatever was in those pictures would prove her brother was innocent."

He crossed to the whiteboard and was studying it while I talked. "Did she say why?"

"Ava said that Alvin never left the festival until well after Dean packed up and left. If I examined all the photos, she was sure I'd see him wandering in the town square. Seems he was looking for Edie and the three of them were supposed to have dinner at the Clam Bake with Mike Shaw."

Without turning around, Dax asked, "But wouldn't that mean that Ava too was still at the festival?"

"That would mean my four main suspects could all alibi each other." I sank against the back of my chair. "I'm right back at square one."

"But are you?" Dax's voice had a clear challenge. "You need to ask more questions about why each of these people had a motive to want Dean Hartley dead."

"Alvin didn't like him dating his sister. Ava didn't want to think her brother killed the man she cared about and she would feel responsible for Alvin leaning into his dark, over-protective mode."

Nodding, Dax said, "What about Shaw and Edie Jenkins?"

"As far as I can tell, Edie didn't have a motive to want him dead, but Mike Shaw wanted to learn Dean's secrets about the new rose he had developed and I would assume, claim it for his own. To top this all off, he wants to buy the business from the Hartley family."

"Then Mike Shaw is back to the top of your suspect list,

and don't forget it might be circumstantial. Lily and I saw him buying new pruners, and his mood was foul. It seems like he had something to hide."

"Mike's always in a bad mood, and I know you've never been out to his place, but the man never puts his tools away; they're scattered everywhere. He's always buying replacements, just ask Tucker."

"Then what about Edie Jenkins? You haven't said much about her."

I looked at her picture on the whiteboard. It was one I had pulled from the garden club website. She was wearing a bright smile, dark sunglasses, and a wide brim hat. The perfect picture of a woman who loved to garden.

"She's a friendly woman, has lived in Pembroke Cove forever. But she doesn't have any family here anymore; they all moved away. Ava is her best friend from what they both said when I talked with them initially, and she seems to spend most of her free time with Ava and her brother."

"You just described the one person who has flown completely under the line of suspicion." Dax picked up a black marker and wrote a big question mark under her picture. "If I were you, I'd take another look at Alvin in conjunction with Edie. Maybe the two of them are romantically involved and they wanted the patent for the roses, and used Ava's relationship with Dean to gain access to his notes. The cameras could have been zoomed in to see him writing them or watching his methods."

"And then they could replicate the procedure and be one step ahead of him to the patent office." I smacked my hand on the table. "That is a distinct possibility, and I never even considered Alvin and Edie in it together." I pushed back from the desk. "I'm going to talk with Alvin again.

Hang around if you want, and I'll fill you in after he confesses the truth."

Dax grinned. "You know, working with you isn't that much of a hardship after all."

I crossed the room and gave him a firm pat on the shoulder. "Once I wrap up this case, I'll make a few calls and see what I can discover that might help your investigation."

"Thanks, and Gage," Dax's voice dropped as he said, "there's nothing between me and Lily. Not that I wouldn't like there to be, but there's not chemistry. I just wanted you to know that. Don't wait too long before asking her out on a real date. You two make a great pair."

I guessed that had to be hard for him to say. "I'm sorry it didn't work out the way you had hoped, but I've loved her most of my life, and I'm going to do all I can to make sure we have a happily ever after just like in the movies, only this will be even better; it will be real."

Dax stuck out his hand. "You're a lucky man."

I spent the next two hours talking first to Alvin and then to Ava, and with each question, it became more apparent they had nothing to do with Dean's death other than the need to protect their sibling. Frustrated with them, I sent them home so I could refocus on Mike Shaw.

Dax was waiting in my office when I walked in. After explaining what a huge time waste questioning the Springs had been, I said, "How about I order in lunch. I'm supposed to meet Lily at two at the greenhouse to look for a lockbox, but I could use a distraction so we could work on your case."

"Sounds good, as long as I'm not holding you up."

"Not at all." I radioed Peabody to see if she and Mac would pick up lunch, and then I called an order into the

Copper Kettle for chowder and sandwiches for Peabody, Mac, as well as me and Dax. Since it was how we usually worked things out, I knew the four of us eating lunch together would give Dax a few more brains on his case.

While we were waiting for lunch, I called Pine Valley to see if Chief Greenleaf had heard any rumblings of people being taken advantage of in real estate transactions and she said she'd check into it and get back to me.

"After we hear from Chief Greenleaf, I'll call Portland and Robin's Pointe to see if there is anything going on. It will be easier for me to get something on the down-low instead of the agency you work for, marching in demanding information."

Dax laughed. "Are you saying I should learn to make less of an entrance when I show up to a new town?"

"Something like that. Your presence can be intimidating at first introduction."

Now he laughed. "Good, just what I like to hear."

"Are you looking forward to getting back to the city?" I asked. I wasn't anxious for him to leave, but when you weren't used to winter weather like we get, it might be a bit much to deal with.

"When I first got here I was, but now small-town life is beginning to grow on me." He went on to tell me about his life in the city and it sounded isolating even with all the people around.

"Maybe you'll want to hang around once the case is over. Who knows, there might be a spot for you on the force, if you're interested."

Peabody and Mac walked past my door. "Lunch, Detectives."

Dax stood. "Let's table that conversation until after I've closed my investigation and you close yours."

· · ·

Over lunch, I filled Peabody and Mac in on what had transpired earlier in the day.

Mac said, "You should definitely take a fresh look at Mike Shaw. He's always been my number one suspect. He's got a lot of anger toward Dean, and their argument was pretty intense at the festival."

"True." I pushed back from the lunch table. "If you want to come out to the Hartley house around two, we're going to look for a lockbox that I'm sure got overlooked." I couldn't explain that a witch had encouraged me to go back. Instead, I said, "That key I found in Brutus' collar indicates Dean was nervous someone might find something important."

Peabody said, "We planned on stopping out and giving you a hand. Remember, you mentioned it when you came in this morning."

"Sorry, this case is bugging me. Every time I think we're closing in, the thread I'm tugging on unravels."

They left, and Dax said, "I'm going to take off too. Thanks for letting me bend your ear today, and I hope you find out something valuable this afternoon."

"Thanks. I do too." I walked in my office and looked at the whiteboard again. I glanced at my phone and saw I had a missed call from Lily. Listening to her voicemail, my blood ran cold as she said, "Hi, Gage. It's about twelve thirty, and Nikki is going with me out to the greenhouse. See, I promised you I wouldn't go alone. I know I'm supposed to meet you there at two, but something is tickling my curiosity. When you're done with the Springs, meet me there. Hopefully by then, I'll have a handle on whatever this is, and I'll tell you all about it. See you later." The phone line went dead.

I checked the time and it was almost two. I hit the speed

dial number, but she didn't answer and it went right to voicemail on the first ring. I grabbed my car keys from the desk and dialed Peabody.

Before she could say a word, I said, "Meet me at the greenhouse and hurry. But no sirens when you get close. Lily could be in danger with the real killer." I wasn't sure why I said that, but every instinct was telling me that Alvin and Ava had just wasted more than half my day with their wild goose chase of confessions and Mike Shaw wasn't the killer either.

Chapter 19
Lily

I walked into Dean's house with Nikki right behind me. I wanted to look at a few things before Gage arrived. If my hunch was correct, Alvin would be cleared by the end of the day even if he had been foolish to confess. But sibling loyalty was admirable. I glanced at Nikki, and she was the closest thing I had to a sister, so I would do the same for her if she was in a tight spot. Our instinct was to protect the people we love most, and at all costs.

The darkness in the small entrance caused me to run my hand over the wall in search of the light switch. I flicked it but nothing happened. Flicking it again, I said, "No light here. Be careful walking around."

Nikki dug into her shoulder bag and withdrew a small penlight and handed it to me. "You go first."

"What? No wand to light the way?"

Nikki smirked. "I didn't bring it out here."

I cautiously took a couple of steps down the hallway and turned into the living room. It was dark like a cemetery on a cloudless night. "It's the middle of the day." I marched over to the windows and pulled back the drapes. Sunlight filled the space, and dust motes danced on the beams streaming through the windows. "That's better."

Nikki looked around the room. "What exactly are we looking for?"

"Pictures, specifically if Dean saved any pictures of him with Alvin, Ava, Mike Shaw, and Edie. They seemed to be a tidy group of five, at least that is how things are shaping up with them having the most invested, not just in Dean's rose business but his death too."

"Do you think it was premeditated, like one of them wanted him dead? Or you know, maybe this is like an Agatha Christie book where through a series of events, multiple people were involved. Like they did it together?"

With my hands resting on my hips, I thought about the idea that everyone was involved in either the death or covering it up, but that didn't seem to fit this case. "No. I think it was an unfortunate accident that played right into one person's long-term scheme."

She gave an involuntary shudder. "That's heartless."

There weren't many framed pictures on the walls. A few prints of roses but nothing with people. I walked into each room and got the same result. What person doesn't even have one family photo on display? Dean had family.

Nikki called from the other room. "Lily. I think I found something." I could hear the excitement in her voice.

I hurried out of the office and into the kitchen where a cabinet was open and a large space on the top shelf was now empty. It looked large enough to have held the box that Nikki was standing in front of, sorting through the contents.

"There is a treasure trove of pictures, old and new." She thrust a stack in my direction. "Those are older but take a look. There's a picture of Dean with Ava and Edie on each side of him, and they're all smiling."

There were pictures of the greenhouse being built with Mike and Alvin grinning broadly while Dean had his arm extended as if saying, welcome to his new business. Then pictures of the inside of the building as it was transformed from a cavernous hulk to the functioning greenhouse it had become.

A few more pictures down, there was the one Nikki had mentioned. Dean had an arm circled around Edie and Ava's waists and they looked happy. I couldn't see a trace of anger as both women's happy faces were captured for posterity on film. I couldn't help but wonder, had Alvin taken the picture? There were several more snapshots of the ladies with Dean, Alvin, and Mike, probably taken the same day based on the clothes and hats they were all wearing. If I hadn't known that someone had turned on Dean, I would have guessed they were all the best of friends.

Nikki peered over my shoulder. "They look so happy."

"Hard to believe one of these people killed him." I flipped through a few more before putting them aside.

She frowned. "Why are you so sure it was one of them? Couldn't it be someone who hasn't shown up on the list of suspects yet?"

I picked up the next stack and thumbed through them while thinking about what I knew of this group of people and said, "Most murders aren't committed by random strangers. More often it is someone you know, if are not friends with. My money is still on Alvin. Remember how he was so angry when we bumped into them?"

"Yeah. I'm sure you're right about him. Alvin probably thought he was protecting Ava. He certainly didn't like that the two were dating. Even though she is a grown woman who can make up her mind about who she wants to spend time with."

I took a long, slow look around the room and knew there were lots of places Dean could have stashed a lockbox. We should have been waiting for Gage when an idea popped into my head. "The key was found in Brutus' collar, right?"

Nikki said, "Yeah. Gage had to use a knife to pry it out."

Snapping my fingers, I said, "Come on. I have an idea."

With Nikki trailing behind me, I hurried to the breezeway which connected the house to the one-car garage.

"What are we looking for?"

I tossed a grin over my shoulder in her direction. "I'm betting he put the box somewhere near where he stores the dog's food. The first clue was in his collar so it should lead to the actual item."

There was a built-in bench on the wall opposite the kitchen, and I could see hinges on the top. My breath caught as I lifted it, full of anticipation. Inside were two large bags of unopened kibble, several leashes, and a box of unopened dog bones. My heart dropped as disappointment slid over me like a veil. I had been so certain.

"You do know there is an easier way for you to find the box." The wide grin on her face had me momentarily perplexed until I knew what she was thinking.

With her eyes focused on me, I nodded. "The location spell." Closing my eyes, with a clear mind, I focused on the tiny gray kitten, who was a replica of Milo. Silently, I said, *I would like to find Dean's lockbox for which Gage has the key. Please show me it's location. As you will, so it shall be.* I waited and bowed my head in the direction of mini Milo who in turn gave me a serene nod. I opened my eyes and waited. This was never an instant resolution, but instead, I needed to allow the spell to work and guide me to where I needed to be. And it suddenly dawned on me. "Nikki, this spell doesn't always work; we never found the straw hat."

"You're right. I wonder why? I've never heard of a spell with an epic fail. Unless it was hidden by magic." She chewed on the tip of her fingernail. "Where to next?"

I didn't like the sound of that, to be coming up against another witch. I straightened my spine. With confidence I didn't feel, I said, "I'm not sure, but I don't believe it's here. Maybe we should head down to the greenhouse." In my mind's eye, a dark box was coming into focus and it looked like it was under a floorboard near the edge of the wall. "I'm pretty sure we'll find it there."

Walking out the back door, I withdrew my phone to call Gage. "That's odd. I don't have any cell service."

Nikki pulled hers out. "Me either. Maybe we're just in a bad area. It will get better as we get closer to the road."

We strolled down the path and the woods were eerily quiet. The other times I had been out here, birds were singing in the trees and the wind rustled the dried leaves on the ground. Despite the warmth of the sun, I felt a chill race down my arms. I glanced at Nikki, and she was running a hand over her arm as if to warm herself. It was a small comfort to know she felt it too. But what on earth could it be?

An overwhelming sense of anger and frustration washed over me, and I stumbled over a rock on the path. Crying out in pain as my ankle twisted, Nikki caught me before I hit the ground.

"Are you alright?"

I grimaced. "Thanks, it's not a big deal."

Worry laced her bright-blue eyes. "We can sit and wait for Gage; you said he was coming out around two."

"That's what he said, but I want to get closer to the greenhouse. It's as if there is a rope that is drawing me closer, and I need to go with it. I'm sure it must be the location spell pulling me to the box."

She held tight to my arm and slipped her arm around my waist. "Then lean on me."

Our pace was slower, but we were making steady progress. As I hobbled from the wood-lined path into the clearing, I noticed an older model sedan in the parking area. I recognized it as belonging to Edie Jenkins. Other than her showing up again unannounced, it was nice to see a friendly face. Maybe it would help shake off the gloom that had begun to wrap around us.

The older woman came around the corner of the greenhouse and waved at us as she took her hat off.

"Oh look, it's Edie." I heard the relief in Nikki's voice, and it matched how I felt, but the sense of dread hadn't abated.

"Hello, girls. I'm surprised to see you out here." She glanced at my ankle, and concern laced her voice. "Lily, are you hurt?"

"It's nothing, a minor sprain. I tripped coming down the path."

She reached my side and took the other arm. "Let me help you inside."

"We'll have to wait outside until Gage gets here. It's locked."

"I was just at the door, and it's open. I guess the police have finished their investigation since Ava confessed today."

I gave her a sharp look. "I think your information is skewed. Alvin confessed."

"No, it's not." Annoyance laced her voice. "I spoke with Ava last night, and she knew that Alvin was going to give himself up to protect her. She decided to come clean and not let her brother take the fall for her misdeeds."

"So it was Ava. It must have been an accident. I feel so bad for them all. Love didn't conquer all in this instance."

Edie gave me a sharp look and then guided us inside the building where the scent of roses wafted through the air. It was comforting despite my discomfort from my ankle. Edie pointed to a bench just inside the door. "Have a seat."

I dropped down and withdrew my cell. "I'm going to give Gage a call and let him know we're not at the house anymore so he can meet us here."

She tipped her head and gave me a side-eyed glance. "That's a good idea. What are you doing out here anyway?"

"Just looking around. You know how I love to satisfy my curiosity." My gaze was drawn to Dean's workbench on the other side of the room and on the floor close by was a bed of blankets that must have been for Brutus. In an instant, I knew under the bedding was where the box was hidden.

"About?" she drawled.

I had to think quick. There was no way I was about to bring her up to speed on the box and I knew Nikki wouldn't say a word. "Roses. There is something about Dean's new hybrid that I wanted to check out."

Edie studied me for a long moment and then gave a forced smile. "He was a talented rose grower."

Nikki asked, "Lily, do you have service yet?"

I looked at my phone. Zero bars. "No, we'll have to use yours."

She shook her head. "My battery died." Nikki looked at Edie. "May we use your phone to call Gage and let him know where to find us? I want to tell him about Lily's sprained ankle."

"Why, of course, Nikki." Her voice had turned to sweet as honey and seemed to be getting more so by the sentence.

Nikki took the phone and said, "One bar. Hopefully the call will go through." She dialed and holding the phone to her ear, she said, "It's not connecting."

"Why don't you drive into town and find Gage. I would hate to have him get concerned if he couldn't find you and Lily at the house. Besides, he should know about the sprain."

Why was she reiterating what Nikki had said about my ankle? It wasn't like it was a compound fracture and I was doubled over in agony.

Nikki surprised me when she said, "That's a great idea. Will you stay with Lily until we get back?"

"What, you're leaving?" I asked.

"I won't be gone long, and Edie can tell you all about these beautiful roses." She gave me a sly wink and that's when I realized I could take the time to find out more about the Ava confession.

"Good idea. We'll be here when you get back."

She placed a comforting hand on my shoulder. "I'll be back in less than an hour."

That was plenty of time to get the details on the Ava and Alvin situation. I handed her the car keys and said to drive careful, but I knew she would.

Edie walked Nikki to the door and closed it behind her. She turned around and put her hat back on and that was when my blood turned to ice and my protection necklace grew hot against my chest. I was in serious trouble.

Chapter 20
Lily

I stood up and hobbled to the center of the greenhouse. There was no place to hide as Edie slowly made her way in my direction. She was wearing the hat from the picture I had found in the house and from the picture at the scene of the murder. Was it possible more than one person had that hat in town? My heart pounded, and I felt like a seal being stalked by a great white shark waiting to have a meal. A chill raced down my spine despite the warm humid air that clung around me. My black tourmaline and amethyst necklace was hot against my skin. This didn't bode well for me. How could I keep Edie talking until Nikki got back with Gage and he could arrest her?

"Nice hat." The words came out like a bullfrog in the marsh.

"Thank you. I can tell by the look on your face you recognize it. A picture of the crime scene perhaps?"

I swallowed hard. "Actually, there's a picture in the house of you, Ava, Mike Shaw, Alvin, and Dean standing together and you're all wearing hats. I remember yours since it is a fedora style. Where did you get it? I'd like to buy one."

"Special mail order and I don't think you'll need a hat where I'm sending you."

I gulped. Dang. Since I had nothing to lose, I said, "I saw that hat near Dean the day he died."

"And I saw you poking around. Guess we both saw things we shouldn't on Saturday." She took a step closer. "But I didn't mean to kill him. He tripped over the ladder and fell on the pruners. When I turned him over, it was an easy decision to leave him there. It solved all my problems. Besides people always believe the worst about me. so why take the chance of doing the right thing?"

"You don't need to do this, Edie," I said, "I'm sure once Gage learns the truth about you and Dean, he'll understand it was just a tragic accident—that Dean tripped, fell onto the garden loppers, and stabbed himself. In fact, I'll be sure to tell him you hadn't wanted Dean to die, that you panicked when you saw the blood and fled the scene."

The woman gave me a cold-blooded smile that did nothing to reassure me I was getting through her crazy thoughts.

"You think you know how it happened, but there was so much more to it, even if it was an unfortunate accident. I was robbed of what should have been mine. All after a casual conversation, Dean dove into grafting roses to develop an ever-blooming variety. It was my idea, not his."

"Did you work on it with him?"

She shook her head. "That isn't the point and don't try to derail this conversation. I don't have all the time in the world to explain this to you."

"What about the pink fingernail?"

A wicked gleam came into her eye and she thrust her chin up. "I dropped it in the grass, and that was a stroke of brilliance. A way to shine the spotlight on Ava and Alvin, and it would have worked if they hadn't been so stupid to confess to save each other.

"When I started trailing you around town and I heard you talking with Tucker about Dean, I knew something had to be done. I always liked you, Lily, even when Ava told me that you were a first-class know-it-all. I defended you. But I was wrong." Her voice was clipped as she said, "And I hate being wrong, about anything. Which is why I'll be doing everyone a favor by putting us all out of any future misery from you."

The best defense was a great offense. I stopped walking backward and stood my ground, hands on hips in a superhero pose. "What, you followed me? I never saw you."

A gleam came into her eye. "Isn't it amazing the talents an old woman can possess?"

Even though I couldn't wrap my head around not noticing I was being followed, I asked, "Was Ava in on your plot to cover up Dean's death?"

She cackled like a wicked witch from an old movie. "No. If you can believe this, Ava was actually in love with the self-centered jerk. She's all boo-hoo, wailing over what she thinks was the loss of her great love. Well, I did her a favor. Dean Hartley was no prize. In time, she'll realize that and thank me."

She took another two steps in my direction with only one row between us. I noticed a bottle filled with brown liquid dangling from her fingers. I was in the middle of the row and figured either way I had time to make an escape even with a bum ankle. After all, I was thirty years younger than her and a witch.

"Did you love him too?" I had to keep her talking and keep my eyes on the soda bottle she had just picked up from the bench. I knew it contained something she planned for me to ingest, but I wasn't about to ask.

A gleam filled her eyes. "That is an interesting question. What do you think?"

"The obvious answer would be yes, but I'm going to say no. Was he your ticket to financial freedom?"

She was nodding and grinned manically. "You are a smart one. How did you come to that conclusion?"

Edie didn't need to know it was an educated guess. Maybe if she believed in my intelligence, she'd stop this insane idea that I needed to die to protect her secret. "It was all about the flowers for you, but I saw the way Dean was smitten with Ava, not you, and that messed up your plan to get your hands on the money."

Her eyes widened for a split second before she said, "No. He never loved anyone or anything except that stupid lug of a dog and of course, money. Besides, the roses were a means to an end for me."

I nodded. "Brutus is a sweet dog, other than a bit on the large size." I was curious about the rose connection. "Did Dean actually create a new hybrid or had he infringed on an existing patent?"

"Does it really matter? You'll be dead soon." She wiggled the bottle with a red cap in the air. "What's in here will take a few weeks to work, but during that time, you're going to be very sick. I hope for your sake you drink more than a sip and let it work its magic."

That was it! There had to be spells that could help me now. I searched my brain. I didn't need to summon Gage; he was already on the way.

"What will happen to me after you force me to drink whatever is in that bottle?" The shiver of fear in my voice was real, but I was confident I'd find a way around this predicament.

"You'll be sick to your stomach and despite feeling cold, you'll sweat profusely. After your handsome detective rushes you to the hospital, they'll give you activated charcoal and pump your stomach, but don't worry, dear. At that point they should provide you with morphine for the pain you'll feel in your esophagus, after that death." She tipped her head and the crazy lurked behind her thick eyelashes. "I do wish I could spare you all of that, but using this herbicide really is the best option. Everyone will understand that you took a drink from this bottle of soda, not realizing what it really was." Her expression drooped into a sad face but there wasn't an ounce of remorse in her voice. "You'll be dead, and I'll be in the clear."

I glanced around the greenhouse, looking for an escape route, but she was between me and both doors. "No one will ever believe I knowingly took a drink of anything from this greenhouse, and Gage will never stop looking for the truth." It was in that moment I wished I had been brave enough to ask him to go on a date with me sooner. I shouldn't have been worrying about rejection or losing his friendship. Gage Erikson had always been the only man for me. Now all I had to do was stay alive until he arrived to arrest Edie.

She gestured to the roses growing. "The best part, I'll have all of this to keep me busy and I promise you on your last breath that I will never harm another living human again." In a flash, she slipped under the bench and was now within arm's length of me.

Edie was a spry lady, and I had to think fast. A big distraction was necessary, and the only one I could think of was a fire. I could light a candle with my breath, but lacking an open flame or a wick, that was not an option. I thought of the spell where I could cause something to break. Would it work on a light bulb, and if that happened could I get a spark to start a small fire? It was my only choice. But how could I break the bulb and create a spark?

Edie waved a finger around my face. "What's going on in that brain of yours? There's no way out, you know."

I noticed a stack of pots behind her. Could I make them float and maybe even fly up and break the bulbs? I split my focus from Edie to the pots, and with a lift of my hand as if I were beginning to conduct an orchestra, they began to float. They had great height and grew closer to the strip of lights.

She turned, her voice shrill. "Are you doing that?"

I didn't waver in my concentration, and with a flick of my wrist, the stack shot up and bounced off the wires that were holding the lights together. With my other hand, I controlled the stack again and tried to get them to hit the light bulb, but I failed again. What was I doing wrong? I could see it in my mind's eye, but it just wasn't working.

Edie took a step closer to me. Was she afraid of the flying pots? Wait, she had that unnerving gleam in her eye again which caused me to lose focus, and the pots crashed to the cement floor. She snapped her fingers and the shards flew up. Oh em gee! She was a witch, and my mediocre skills were no match for someone with years of experience.

Now it came down to her wits pitted against mine. Her arm stretched out and sliced the air in front of me. I stepped back and stumbled, falling against the wooden bench. Grabbing a handful of potting soil, I threw it in her face and began to move as fast as I could hobble in the opposite direction. Edie didn't move quick enough, and I made my mark.

As she wiped the dirt from her eyes, rage filled her face,

and sputtering a few words I didn't understand, she finally shouted, "Stop!"

But I took this opportunity to put into action the last spell I had been working on, making an object appear as if it had vanished. The only unknown is would she still feel the bottle in her hand? Before I spoke the incantation of the disappearing spell, with a flick of the wrist I sent pots of flowers dancing in the air. Another distraction was always a good idea when trying to escape a killer. Flower pots bounced on the workbench top and back into the air again. It would have looked comical if the situation wasn't dire. She was batting at the pots and commanding for them to stop. I didn't waste a moment, stating the spell loud and clear. "I banish the small bottle which is in your hand. I vanish the bottle into the air. So, banish and vanish I do decree, and so it shall be." I knew I didn't have the words right, but I didn't care. Clapping my hands together, the bottle flew from her hand and hit the wall on the other side of the greenhouse. It wasn't exactly what I had intended but there was enough distance between me and the bottle that I relaxed for a brief instant.

The door burst open, and Gage tumbled in with Peabody and Mac on his heels while Nikki hovered in the doorway. "Freeze!" His voice held an unmistakable air of authority, and Edie dropped her hands as I took that moment to picture the flower pots sitting in neat rows on the bench, pressing my hands in a downward motion. Much to my surprise, Gage didn't seem to notice anything unusual about the flowers or the pots.

Sharon rushed up behind Gage and seized Edie by the upper arm. "I'm placing you under arrest for the murder of Dean Hartley." Her gaze flicked to me. "Are you okay?"

I nodded as my breath began to return to normal.

Pointing beyond the bench at the back wall, I said, "There is a plastic bottle over there with poison in it. She was planning on forcing me to drink it." I shuddered just thinking about how close I had come this time.

"I stand corrected, Ms. Jenkins. Murder and attempted murder." She glared at Edie. "Mac, get the bottle and bag it as evidence."

Edie glowered at me, and I was shocked to see not an ounce of remorse in them. "Lily, you are a worthy amateur witch."

"Wait!"

Gage took her arm and Sharon moved to help Mac. He looked at me. "What is it?"

I dropped my voice for her ears only. "Edie, did you use an invisibility spell to follow me and what did you do at my bookstore today?"

Her eyes narrowed, but she gave me a crazy smile. "But of course, my dear girl, and good luck undoing my spell. Oh, and one last thing, you should teach your familiar to mind his manners; he was quite rude to me when I was in your store."

I furrowed my brow. "What are you talking about?"

"That fleabag said that I shouldn't be rough when all I was doing was petting him. Downright rude."

Gage gave me a questioning look and I nodded. "I'm done."

Sharon came back over and steered Edie to the door while Mac bagged the bottle. "All clear, Detective. We'll transport Ms. Jenkins and meet you at the station."

With one nod, Gage then turned and pulled me into his arms before letting me go and giving me his full attention. His sharp gaze took in my appearance from my toes to my head. "You're not hurt?"

I shook my head, not trusting myself to speak yet.

"I am so sorry it took me so long to get here. None of the police cars would start; it was the most bizarre thing. And Peabody told me the cell phones didn't work, and then Nikki showed up. Once I told her of the issue, she took matters into her own hands and the cars started." He wrapped his arms around me again and his voice was muffled as he held me close. "Edie just called you a witch in front of Mac and Peabody and confessed to casting spells."

"I know. Hopefully, they'll just chalk it up to ravings of a madwoman, but yes, she knew. Not that it matters. I was able to best her, at least to buy enough time for you to arrive." I inhaled the smell of coffee and cookies and I smiled to myself. This was the best part of my day.

"Edie is a witch." He didn't ask but made a simple statement.

"Yes. Where's Nikki? Is she okay?"

"She's fine and waiting outside. She might want us to have a couple of minutes alone."

"Gage." I pulled away to put distance between us. "Will you walk outside with me? This place gives me the creeps."

He smiled and reached for my hand. "I agree. But you can tell me what happened while taking a stroll, and then I have to get back to town and make sure Edie is locked up tight." He tipped his head. "I might need to check with my mom or your aunt Mimi. If she's a witch, do you think she could escape?"

"I have no idea, but that might not be a bad idea, bring in the superpowers. After all, you heard Edie; I'm just an amateur witch."

His hand fit in mine just right, and I was even more certain about what I wanted to happen next.

Once we were outside in the late afternoon, he said, "When did Edie show up and why?"

"She's been following me for the last couple of days and using some kind of spell so I didn't see her, and then she heard Tucker tell me that Dean bought the new pruners and Edie had stopped in right after him. That made her think that I had figured everything out. Of course, it wasn't until we got here and she started ranting about the injustice of life did the whole story come tumbling out." I squeezed his hand. "It's sad really. They argued, Dean tripped and fell on the pruners. She turned him over and left him there, saying she didn't call for help because she was sure people would accuse her." I gave a wry laugh. "Guess that idea didn't pan out so well because now we know she is responsible for his death. Even if she didn't do something deliberate to start, she was pleased with the outcome. Walking away while a man bleeds to death and not calling for help is criminal. And she felt Dean was a loser, especially when it seemed he liked Ava, and we can't forget they were fighting over money for the new rose variety he was going to patent. Dean wasn't the bad guy here. But my guess, Edie spread enough gossip for the garden club members to think he was."

Gage dropped my hand and slung his arm around my waist. I stopped walking and slipped from his half embrace.

I took a deep breath and shook out my shoulders like a boxer squaring up for a prize fight, still remembering how I felt when I realized she was a witch. "I hope Sharon and Mac can handle her. I have no idea how strong her magic is."

"I'll let you in on a little secret. Mom comes by the station from time to time and adds protection spells for the people working there. It's her way of dealing with the fact that I'm in law enforcement with zero magic."

"She's doing what she can." I had to wonder if Aunt Mimi had done similar types of things to the bookshop before I discovered that I was a witch. I could ask her, but instead I'd see what I might do to protect the shop and maybe even figure out why the light bulbs kept burning out. "I'll bet that was Edie's spell on my shop. As an added bonus for her to annoy me."

"What are you saying?"

"The light bulbs burning out and books flying off the shelves—it had to be Edie that caused all of that. I won't need to call the electrician; I just need to protect my store with my own magic."

"Maybe your book and Milo can help you with that."

I cupped his cheek with my hand, ready to change the subject. "I'm thrilled we're going to have our first official date on Saturday, but there's one thing I want to be perfectly clear on."

Gage's smile was slowly becoming a wide grin. "And what is that?"

"Having coffee with Dax was like having coffee with Aunt Mimi. I do consider him a friend and I hope that won't be awkward since I got the vibe he viewed me as a bit more."

"How could he not? You're an amazing woman—smart, well read, loyal, active in the community, and a very good friend too."

I felt my face grow warm. "You just described Milo."

He laughed. "You're also beautiful and he saw you for more than I wanted to admit to myself. In truth, I owe him my thanks. It was his interest in you that made me decide to take a chance." He brushed my bangs back from my eyes.

"If you hadn't been honest with me about how you felt, I was ready to tell you. Three times in a few months you've come close to a serious situation and if that hasn't taught me anything, well, nothing ever will. However, there is one thing I'd like to ask."

"And what's that?" I took his hand.

"If you decide to insert yourself in my next case, don't come in close proximity to any of my suspects."

I tipped my head. "Now where is the fun in that?"

He looked into my eyes. "I'm willing to risk our friendship to date you. But I'm not willing to put you in harm's way so you can solve a case."

There was an intensity I hadn't seen in his eyes before. "I'll be more careful next time."

He chuckled softly. "Then you'd better keep reading that book of yours."

I groaned. "Now you sound like Milo and Aunt Mimi."

"At least I'm in good company." He brushed his lips over mine, and I felt a spark. Was it my magic sizzling or something more?

"I am looking forward to having dinner with you." His eyes sparkled as he said, "And I felt that zing too."

I chuckled softly and whispered, "Maybe I've cast a spell over you. I am a witch after all."

He laughed and pulled me close in his arms. "What we have is magic."

If you loved Tea & Trouble help other readers find this book: **Please leave a review now!**
Are you ready to read more from the Lily and the gang in Pembroke?

Keep reading for a sneak peek at

Scares & Dares
A Book Store Cozy Mystery Series
Order Now
Or
Shop at Lucinda Race

Not ready to stop reading yet? If you sign up for my newsletter at www.lucindarace.com/newsletter you will receive an excerpt for Cookies & Capers, the introduction of when Lily met Milo right away as my thank-you gift for choosing to get my newsletter.

Scares & Dares

A BOOK STORE COZY MYSTERY

Book Four

LUCINDA RACE

Chapter One - Lily

"Halloween is four days away." Pointing at the calendar on the wall, I looked around my kitchen at my boyfriend, Gage; my best friend, Nikki; and her guy, Steve, who were relaxing around my table. We were done stuffing our faces with meat lovers and extra-cheese pizza. "I know it's late in the game, but we've been tasked with taking over decorating and running the haunted house on All Hallows Eve. But if we're going to be successful, we have to come up with a fool-proof plan. Everyone in Pembroke Cove expects to be scared out of their boots after dark. So, we need to have two versions, one for the kiddos and an adult-orientated theme."

Gage ran his finger around the edge of his glass. "That doesn't give us much time to bring in volunteers and build the sets. I can reach out to Corbin Marks, and maybe with a little help from our favorite witches, my mom and your Aunt Mimi, along with you ladies, we can get it done in plenty of time."

My familiar, Milo, stalked into the room and looked at the two dogs—Brutus, a great Dane Gage had adopted and Murphy, Nikki's retriever—snoozing in front of the door.

"My dear witch," he grumbled good-naturedly, "you should have told me we were having guests. It appears I've snoozed through most of the fun if the sleeping dogs are any indication of what happened in here."

Over the last few months, I had gotten used to my cat talking to me and the only person in the room who could hear him besides me was Nikki. Both Gage and Steve were non-magical and what they heard was Milo meowing whenever he spoke. I scooped him off the floor and held him close to my chest, nuzzling his head. "We're planning the haunted house. Any good ideas?"

"Now, why would I have any thoughts on that subject. I don't like anything that is scary. Humans are looking to get spooked when they don't even realize right in their own backyards are witches, wizards, and a few other paranormal creatures."

I gently turned his head to look at me. "Wait? What did you say?"

Milo tapped my cheek with his soft paw. "Put me down on the floor. I have things to do and if you would read more of your book, *Practical Beginnings*, you'd know all that our little town has to offer." He did little to keep the frustration from his voice.

Before I did as he asked, I had to know, "What do you mean others?"

"That's for me to know and you to find out." He wriggled out of my hands and stalked from the room without a backward glance.

Gage gestured to Milo's retreating form. "What was that all about?"

"My familiar just informed me there are other paranormal beings living in Pembroke Cove and not just witches and wizards." I gave Nikki a sharp look. "Did you know this?"

She shrugged but didn't look at me. "It's no big deal and nothing to worry about. Most of the time it's just witches and the occasional wizard hanging out, and if anyone does come around, it's in the spring."

With her noncommittal response, I figured it was a topic of conversation left for another day, especially if we have five or six months before anyone showed up. But what kind of paranormals could there be? Maybe my book, *Practical Beginnings*, would shed some light on the topic. And when the guys weren't around, I could get Nikki to open up.

"Alright then, let's talk about what we can use from last year." I got up and grabbed my laptop from the counter and sat back down. "I talked to Alice and Bea who were both on the committee last year, and Bea sent me some pictures of what they stored in the shed at the animal shelter." I tapped a few keys and turned the screen so my friends could see it. "We're going to hold it at the grange hall like it's been in past years, but I'm hoping we can have a hay bale walkway and place some skeletons around with spooky music and cobwebs. In the entrance we could have a mural that looks like an old mansion with ripped wallpaper that has fallen into disrepair or something." My ideas were starting to flow so I kept going. "Then we can have areas with different scenes; some will have people as props, like the table with the domed platter and when the dome comes off, it's just a talking head. It goes without saying spooky music and spiderwebs are everywhere inside. Then I'll ask if Aunt Mimi could have a witch area with a cauldron, stirring up potions, and Nate could be her ghoul."

Nikki grinned. "They'll jump at the chance."

I nodded. "I'd like to have a couple of vampires popping out of coffins, a mummy or two that's animated or real, and maybe some people in armor that move around to scare folks."

Gage rubbed his hands together. "A magic mirror and crystal ball are both good options. My mom would be happy to help."

My enthusiasm seemed to be contagious.

Steve said, "What about doors opening and closing and candles everywhere?"

"Battery operated," Gage interjected. "We don't want to have to call the fire company. If we don't get enough volunteers, the animated props can fill in where we don't have live bodies too."

"There should be jack-o'-lanterns everywhere. I'll bet Marshall Stone will donate to the cause and maybe he'll even help carve." Nikki sighed. "I love carving faces."

"I'm sure with your kitchen witch abilities, they're a work of art." I snapped my fingers as my gaze slid to my witchcraft book. "We need a fake spell book that opens and closes on its own; Aunt Mimi can cast a spell for that. Maybe with a funny, but fake incantation on the page in case someone reads it."

Nodding, Gage said, "Some well-placed lifelike rats and other critters that move, covered with glow-in-the-dark paint. And I'll even buy some roses for my girl and she can let them die before using them at the entrance of the haunted house."

I could feel the frown appear when I remembered our most recent death in town where the local rose grower had been killed. But I didn't say anything to cause anyone to go down that sad path. "I think we have a lot of good ideas.

Let's write them down and see who we can line up to donate or volunteer to help."

Gage went to the pantry closet and pulled out my clue chalkboard. A chill raced over my arms when I thought about the last few times I had used it, for the three murders in town. But this time it was going to be used for a happy occasion and that would kick the bad vibes right to the curb.

"Good idea. We can take pictures on our phone so if you find something that will work, text me and I'll add the information to our master list." I took the chalk from Gage's fingers and jotted down all the ideas we had come up with.

Nikki surveyed the list and smiled. "This is a good start. Now let's see about getting people to help. Like Lily said, we don't have a lot of time to make this happen and I want to do all we can to give this town the most memorable haunted house ever."

I flashed Gage a look. "Do you think Dax will help out since his investigation seems to have gone cold?" Dax Peters was the most recent, temporary transplant to our small town. He was a big city federal investigator on the trail of a real estate scheme that had infiltrated and had, in some ways, been responsible for two people dying in Pembroke Cove. The head librarian had been forcing people, who had secrets to hide, to pay bribes, and then a real estate agent was swindling people out of profits from selling their homes. All for hefty kickbacks from an unknown Mr. Big. Squaring my shoulders, I pushed all of those worries from my mind. We had fun to focus on and lots of it. The kids both young and old alike were looking forward to the haunted house.

Gage tapped out a text on his phone and it quickly pinged with an incoming message. He grinned. "Dax loves

Halloween and he'd love to help. Should I ask him to come over?"

I looked at our tiny committee of three plus me. "The more the merrier but see if he'll swing by The Sweet Spot and pick up a box of pastries if they're still open. I'll make coffee."

Nikki smiled. "If I had known your sweet tooth was kicking in and you wanted dessert, I would have baked."

Glancing at the wall clock, I saw it was after they typically closed. "On second thought, just tell him to come on over. William will be closed by now."

With a quick nod, Gage set his phone aside. "Dax should be here in about fifteen minutes."

"Has he finally moved out of the motel?" Steve asked.

"Not yet, but last week, when he stopped in the bookstore, I asked him if he was thinking about making our little cove a permanent home, but he's still on the fence. I'm sure it's hard to uproot your life and move from a place where you live an anonymous life to a place where everyone knows when you sneeze."

Gage raised an eyebrow as if asking me to expand on my conversation with Dax. I shrugged and said, "It was no big deal. With no leads to follow up on, he's been reading a lot more."

"There is a library," Gage grumbled and I had to smile.

"Green has never been your color." I dropped a kiss on his cheek before getting up to start the coffee.

Nikki joined me. "I'll rustle up something sweet."

Steve leaned back in his chair and grinned. "Sometimes it's great being engaged to a witch."

I dropped the glass carafe in the sink and didn't care if it broke. "You're engaged? Why didn't you tell me?"

"Steve and I decided we'd work it into the conversation. It just happened this morning when I was up to my elbows in pie crust. It was so romantic." A dreamy look floated over her face and she withdrew a stunning diamond ring from her jeans pocket and slipped it on her finger before placing her left hand over her heart. "Isn't it beautiful?"

Gage got up and hugged Nikki and then vigorously shook Steve's hand. "Congratulations. You're one lucky guy."

"Don't I know it." He wiggled his eyebrows and said, "Jump in; the water's like a hot tub in winter."

I couldn't help but snort. "It took us fifteen years after we graduated college to go on our first date just a couple of weeks ago. We are *so* not ready to jump in and get engaged."

Nikki gave me a long look. "You and Gage have been better friends than most married couples I know, and that is the basis of a good marriage. Look at me and Steve. It took us a long time to let our friendship develop into love and now we're getting married." She grabbed my hands. "Please tell me you'll be my maid of honor?"

Throwing my arms around her, I held her close. "Just try and stop me."

Steve said, "Gage. Any chance you'd stand up for me?"

Gage clapped him on the shoulder. "No place I'd rather be."

Nikki giggled. "We haven't set the date yet but probably spring or summer."

Steve said, "Or sooner if I can convince my future wife to agree."

I overlooked that comment. "Like when we get paranormal company?" I hoped my question would prompt a response.

She clasped my hand. "Stop worrying about what may

or might not happen. We should all have dinner on Friday and start talking about wedding plans."

I looked at Gage, and he said, "I'm free."

Taking his hand and grinning at Nikki and Steve, I said, "Then we have our first official wedding planning night."

A knock at the door stopped the conversation and with a flick of her wrist, Nikki had a pumpkin cheesecake sitting on the counter. She gave me one of those smiles when she wasn't trying to show off how strong her magic was and mine wasn't. "It's no big deal; I just summoned it from my house to yours."

Gage opened the door for Dax.

He held up a hand in greeting. In his soft Southern drawl, he said, "Hey, everyone. Thanks for including me. Halloween is my favorite holiday." He spotted the cheesecake on the counter and grinned. "Just in time for dessert too."

I glanced at the sink and was relieved to see the carafe was in one piece after dropping it. "Come in. I was just making coffee and we can talk about plans for the big event."

He pulled up a chair and sat down at the table, then noticed the open laptop. Glancing at this list, he said, "Impressive. But is there enough time to get this all done and ready in three days? You can't count the day it opens to still be constructing the scenes. Then it's all about the finishing touches."

Gage grinned. "You have no idea what these ladies can do when they put their minds to it and we have a list of volunteers to help too. Mine and Lily's parents will pitch in as well as her aunt and Nate."

Nikki said, "My parents don't live in Pembroke Cove anymore, but Steve's family will help."

Steve took her hand and grinned. "Yeah, especially after we tell them our news. Everyone is going to want to be around."

Dax looked around our group. "News?"

"I popped the question to my lovely Nikki and she said yes."

I swear if Steve were a witch, he'd be floating, and I knew that was possible based on what I had read in my book.

"That's great. Congratulations to both of you." His smile was wide, but there was a bit of sadness lingering in his eyes. Could it be he was still feeling like he was on the outside looking in? Hopefully working on this event would change all that.

With the coffee pot turned on, I sat in the chair next to Gage. "Dax, tell us, do you want to be in a scene or just behind them?"

He sat up straight in the chair and grinned. "Are you kidding? I want to be a vampire lying in a coffin."

I couldn't help but shudder. There was something about the lore of vampires and vampire-themed movies that set my teeth on edge. I mustered up enthusiasm to say, "That's one way to scare people coming through, but only after we finish with the kiddos. I don't want to give a youngster the fright of their lives."

A Free Story for You

Have you enjoyed Tea & Trouble? Not ready to stop reading yet? If you sign up for my newsletter at www.lucindarace.com/newsletter you will received Cookies & Capers which is the start of Lily and Milo's adventure as my thank-you gift for choosing to get my newsletter.

Cookies & Capers

I stood in front of the old wood and glass door as I pocketed the keys to the Cozy Nook Bookshop. Aunt Mimi had signed her bookstore over to me. She said it felt like giving me her baby. But I loved the shop as much as my aunt did. We had worked together for the last twelve years. After attending the University of Maine, I had a degree in history and education. I had always wanted to be a teacher, but jobs were scarce and after substituting for a few years, I moved back to my hometown of Pembroke, Maine, and Aunt Mimi hired me as soon as I unpacked my suitcase.

Spending time with my aunt, learning the business, had been the best experience. I offered to buy the shop when she wanted to retire, but she wouldn't hear of it. As long as she had free books for life, and her long-term boyfriend Nate, she said it was a fair deal. From my point of view, I had built-in backup for years to come.

Now that I was the bookshop owner, Aunt Mimi was no longer coming in every day which meant her cat, Phoenix, wasn't either and the space felt empty without a kitty lying in the window or skulking about as kitties do. I was off to the Pembroke Animal Palace to see if I could find a match.

It was a short walk in the bright noonday sun. The spring air from the ocean carried a tang of salt, but the breeze was refreshing. I waved to one of my best friends, Gage Erikson, as he drove past in his police-issued sedan. My heart fluttered in my chest.

He was a detective on the force. Not that we had much crime in our small seaside town. But one of these days I was going to get brave and tell him I had been carrying a torch for him since we were in ninth grade. What's the worst thing that could happen? We'd still be best friends, right?

I continued down the brick sidewalk, waving to William North from the Sweet Spot Bakery. He was sweeping the area around the small bistro tables in front of the bakery. William was wearing a large pristine white apron and a wide smile. A deep inhale confirmed my suspicion. He was baking cookies. My mouth watered. I did a half turn and went back to where he was finishing up. "Good morning, William." I bobbed my head in the shop's direction. "What is that tantalizing smell?"

He held open the brightly polished glass door. "One of your favorites, Lily. Chocolate chip and pecan cookies. Can I interest you in one before you continue on your mission?"

I gave him a side-look. "Mission?"

He chuckled. "Over the years my Lulu had said you

had two speeds, strolling and purposeful. Just now it was purposeful so hence you're on a mission."

"I'm going to the shelter, hoping to find a kitty. The shop is lonely now that Phoenix is home every day with Aunt Mimi, and I think a cat napping in the window adds an air of serenity to the place."

"Unless you're allergic."

He had a point, but I was not willing to be deterred. I smiled. "I'm always happy to deliver to a customer." I leaned over the glass bakery case, like a kid pressing her nose against the candy case. "You made sugar cookies too and frosted them?" I sighed. I was going to need to exercise more if he continued to bake all my favorites. He was smiling at me as I looked up. "Are the chocolate pecan ready?"

He wiggled his eyebrows. "I have a tray cooling in the back."

"Then can I have one of those and a sugar cookie, but to go?"

With a flick of his wrist, he snapped open a white bakery bag and called over his shoulder. "Jerilyn, would you please bring out the last batch of cookies?"

I heard a muffled, coming, and smiled. "It's good that Jerilyn stayed on." I said nothing about his beloved wife Lulu. Rumor had it she was ill and not doing well.

He nodded. "It is. She's a hard worker and excellent with the customers."

Jerilyn bustled in from the back room carrying a large stainless-steel tray. It was lined with parchment paper and cookies the size of the palm of my hand. It was going to taste so good with a hot cup of tea later.

William put two in the bag, along with two sugar cookies, and then he handed it to me. I paid for my cookies and thanked him. "Stop by the shop later. You might just get to meet my new fur baby."

"Sounds like a plan." He grinned and crossed his arms over his rounded midsection. "You're more like your aunt than you realize. Ever since she opened that bookshop, she's had a cat, too."

I paused, tucked the bakery bag in my tote, and with my hand on the door, I turned and gave him a wide grin. "And now it's time I carry on the tradition." With a jaunty wave, I called, "Wish me luck."

Cookies & Capers is only available by signing up for my newsletter – sign up for it here at www.lucindarace.com/newsletter

Love to Read?

**All ebooks and signed paperback copies can be
ordered from my website at:
Shop at Lucinda Race**

Cozy Mystery Books
A Bookstore Cozy Mystery Series 2023
***Welcome to Pembroke Cove, where witches and
murders are multiplying…***
Books & Bribes
*It was an ordinary day until the book of Practical Magic
conked Lily on the head causing her to see stars. And then
she discovered her cat, Milo, could talk.*

Catnaps & Crimes
A witch, a snarky familiar and murder…

Tea & Trouble
*When reading tea leaves turns to murder can Lily solve this
latest case?*

Love to Read?

Scares & Dares
What does a haunted house and murder have in common?
New witch Lily Michaels is determined to solve the case.

Holidays & Homicide
Even a fun event like the annual Glow & Glide can lose its
charm when a body is discovered on the ice.

Leprechauns & Larceny
A leprechaun, a wedding, and pirate treasure, Oh My!

Magicians & Murder
When four magicians roll into town for a show more than
fun is on one person's mind.

Artifacts & Amulets Summer 2024
Milo has been keeping secrets, which can be deadly.

Cranberries & Criminals November 2024

Cowboys of River Junction

Second Chances in Montana
Twenty years later Renee and Hank are back where they fell
in love, but reality is like a spring frost and is a long-distance
relationship their only option for their second chance?

Stars Over Montana
The cowboy broke her heart but he never stopped loving her.
Now she's back ready to run her grandfather's ranch...

Hiding in Montana
Can love flourish while danger lurks in the shadow?

Love to Read?

Moonlight Over Montana
*Will a single mom find love with the handsome cowboy who
saved her and her daughter from danger?*

The Sandy Bay Series
<u>Sundaes on Sunday</u>
*A widowed school teacher and the airline pilot whose little
girl is determined to bring her daddy and the lady from the
ice cream shop together for a second chance at love.*

Last Man Standing/Always a Bridesmaid
<u>Barrett</u>
Has the last man standing finally met his match?

<u>Marie</u>
*Career-focused city girl discovers small-town charm can lead
to love.*

Price Family Series
<u>Breathe</u>
Her dream come true may be the end of his...
Crush
The first time they met was fleeting, the second time
restarted her heart.
<u>Blush</u>
*He's always loved her, but he left. Now he's back...the
question, does she still love him?*
<u>Vintage</u>
He's an unexpected distraction, she gets his engine running...
<u>Bouquet</u>
*Sweet second chances for a widow and the handsome
billionaire...*

Social Media

Follow Me on Social Media

Like my Facebook page
Join Lucinda's Heart Racer's Reader Group on Facebook
Twitter @lucindarace
Instagram @lucindaraceauthor
BookBub
Goodreads
Pinterest

About the Author

Award-winning and best-selling author Lucinda Race is a lifelong fan of reading. As a young girl, she spent hours reading novels and getting lost in the fun and hope they represent. While her friends dreamed of becoming doctors and engineers, her dreams were to become a writer—a novelist.

As life twisted and turned, she found herself writing nonfiction but longed to turn to her true passion. After developing the storyline for A McKenna Family Romance, it was time to start living her dream. Her fingers practically fly over computer keys as she weaves stories of mystery and romance.

Lucinda lives with her two little dogs, a miniature long hair dachshund and a shih tzu mix rescue, in the rolling hills of western Massachusetts. When she's not at her day job, she's immersed in her fictional worlds. And if she's not writing romance or cozy mystery novels, she's reading everything she can get her hands on.